A Ponderosa Resort
Romantic Comedy

Sergeant
SEXYPANTS

USA Today Bestselling Author
TAWNA FENSKE

SERGEANT SEXYPANTS

A PONDEROSA RESORT ROMANTIC COMEDY

TAWNA FENSKE

Bree Bracelyn doesn't date cops. It's a personal rule that quavers when Austin Dugan flashes his baby blues—and his badge—at Ponderosa Resort's grand opening. Bree's the family fixer, running the resort's PR and her siblings' lives with cheerful efficiency. But one thing in Bree's past can't ever be fixed, which is why she's staying the hell away from Officer Hottie.

Austin's heart tacks up a wanted poster with Bree's name the instant he lays eyes on her. Okay, the no-cops rule is an obstacle, but not impossible for a guy ambitious enough to be a shoo-in as the next police chief. Besides, he knows Bree's into him, whether they're flirting over weird flatware or getting frisky in the front seat of his vintage Volvo.

As Bree and Austin bond over cupcakes and hot springs hookups, Bree knows it's a matter of time before the skeletons in her closet topple into a messy heap on Austin's squeaky-clean life. Is there hope for a happy ending, or will their love end up DOA?

ALSO IN THE PONDEROSA RESORT ROMANTIC COMEDY SERIES

- Studmuffin Santa
- Chef Sugarlips
- Sergeant Sexypants
- Hottie Lumberjack
- Stiff Suit
- Mancandy Crush (novella)
- Captain Dreamboat
- Snowbound Squeeze (novella)
- Dr. Hot Stuff (coming soon!)

If you dig the Ponderosa Resort books, you might also like my Juniper Ridge Romantic Comedy Series. There's even some crossover with characters featured in both worlds. Check it out here:

- Show Time
- Let It Show (coming March 2021!)
- Show Down (coming soon!)
- Just for Show (coming soon!)

- Show and Tell (coming soon!)
- Show of Hands (coming soon!)

For my readers.
Thank you for loving these characters as much as I do.
Is it creepy that we've all seen them naked?

CHAPTER 1

AUSTIN

"*I*t really would be your most noble, heroic act."

Mrs. Sampson beams and adjusts the glasses perched halo-style in her salt-and-pepper perm, then folds her hands on the bistro table like she's delivered the closing argument in a murder trial.

I fix her with my best cop stare, which loses some impact since I'm holding a plate of shrimp puffs. "I rescued your cat off the roof two weeks ago, Mrs. S," I remind her, ignoring the fact that my job also involves chasing down the occasional bad guy. "But *this* would be my most heroic act?"

She nods like I've finally gotten a question right on an algebra test, which is fitting since she was my middle school math teacher. She lifts her glass of champagne, sloshing some into the manicured grass. "Exactly," she says. "It means so much to the children."

I take a calming breath and remind myself she's an old lady. An old lady who just stroked my bicep, but still an old lady.

"Taking off my shirt means so much to the children." I set down my plate and try the cop stare again. This time, she blushes.

"It's for charity," she says. "People love those calendars that

1

have pictures of real policemen with their clothes off and something covering up their—" she clears her throat dramatically, "—*unmentionables*."

Good God, we need a subject change. "If you're mentioning the unmentionables, haven't we already defeated the purpose?"

She ignores me and squeezes my bicep again. "You'd be perfect for January, sweetheart, with those pretty blue eyes, and maybe you'd pose shirtless on a dogsled with no pants but your police hat over your—"

"Okay, no." I brace my hands on the table. "The department has policies about police officers being photographed in uniform." Admittedly, I don't remember a code about not using one's peaked cap to cover one's junk, but that's beside the point. "Following the rules is kinda my job, Mrs. Sampson."

She looks at me like I've just announced a fondness for rolling naked in lime Jell-O and gives a sad little head shake. "You're in line to become the next chief of police," she says slowly, like I might have forgotten. "Don't you *make* the rules?"

I open my mouth to explain that my promotion from sergeant to lieutenant is no guarantee I'll be head honcho when the chief retires, even though everyone's acting like it's a foregone conclusion. Before I get a word out, my father strides over in his sheriff's uniform and claps me on the shoulder while turning his election-year grin on Mrs. Sampson.

"Judy," he says. "You're looking radiant."

"Thank you, John," she says, preening. "Would you please tell your son to take his clothes off for the children?"

My father frowns and rubs a hand over his chin. "Well, I can't rightly suggest that as a good career move, but—"

"For charity," she interrupts, increasingly impatient.

I fight the urge to roll my eyes, wondering what was coming after my father's "but." Is there a situation in which he'd advise me to get naked for minors?

Mrs. Sampson is still prattling on about the charity calendar, so I tune them out and start surveying the crowd. There must be a hundred people milling around the expansive lawn at Ponderosa Luxury Ranch Resort on this warm fall afternoon. Some of them linger by the fire pits, laughing in sundresses and swirls of wood smoke, while others chatter by the buffet tables, pretending it's totally in their normal wheelhouse to eat herbed squash confit made by a famous Michelin-starred chef.

Most are faces I recognize, all here to celebrate the opening of this fancy new playground for the wealthy. Not that I'm complaining. It's great for the local economy and all, but I feel weird hobnobbing at an event meant for VIPs and dignitaries and other local elite.

I'm hardly a VIP, but the uniform and job title nabbed me the invitation, so here I am. I pick up a shrimp puff and shove it in my mouth as my father interrupts my reverie.

"Don't you think so, son?"

I turn back to him, debating whether to bluff or come clean that I lost track of the conversation. "What's that, dad?"

My father smiles like I passed some kind of test, and I'm betting he read my mind. He knows I don't have it in me to bluff, which isn't a bad thing. My straight-shooting, rule-abiding approach to life makes me a damn good cop.

"Just saying that the Ryan Zonski case stands a good chance of being overturned if it ends up going before the Oregon Court of Appeals," he says. "You'd be right in the thick of it again."

I resist the urge to grit my teeth at the prospect of having my worst case reopened. "Let's hope not," I offer mildly. "The new DA loves settling out of court. I'd hate to see the victim's family go through that again."

Mrs. Sampson gives a sad little head shake. "Such an awful tragedy."

I'm wracking my brain for a good subject change when an angel glides into my line of sight.

She's making a beeline for us, this angel with dark curls and wide green eyes. She can't be more than five feet tall, but there's a fierceness in her expression suggesting she'd cheerfully junk-punch anyone who crossed her. It's an interesting contrast to the bright smile she offers as she approaches our table in a slim blue dress that hugs her curves. I do my best not to stare, but holy marshmallows, she's stunning.

"Marshmallows?" She looks at me and cocks her head.

Oh shit. Did I say that out loud?

"I—uh—"

"I'd love one." My father reaches for her, and I consider elbowing him in the ribs when I see she's clutching a fistful of skewers. Each one is threaded with a massive, pillowy marshmallow that looks homemade. Not that I know what a home-made marshmallow looks like, but these aren't the Jet-Puffed confections of my Boy Scout years.

"You'll find homemade graham crackers and Maison Pierre Marcolini chocolates on trays beside all the fire pits," she adds, brushing a dark curl from her forehead. "Help yourself to anything you need to make the perfect s'mores."

Good Lord, she has a beautiful mouth. That's never been the first thing I've noticed in a woman, but I can't stop staring at hers. Those lush, rosebud lips that look softer than—than—okay, I was going to say marshmallows again, which means she's zapped most of the vocabulary from my brain.

Her gaze shifts to mine and locks, and I swear she just read my thoughts. I can't tell whether she's intrigued or annoyed, but the wheels are turning in her head.

I stick out my hand. "Sergeant Austin Dugan, Bend PD."

There's a moment of awkwardness when she's forced to shift the fistful of skewers to her left hand, but the instant her palm slides against mine, a flame bursts in the center of my chest. I won't need a fire pit to turn this marshmallow to a puddle of goo.

"Bree Bracelyn," she says. "I'm the Vice President of

Marketing and Events for Ponderosa Resort. Thank you so much for joining us."

"My pleasure." The word *pleasure* rolls off my tongue with a more porny tone than I intended, or maybe that's all in my head. I haven't released her hand yet, so I should probably do that.

The instant I let go, my father extends his own handshake. "John Dugan, I'm the sheriff out here." My dad gives Bree's hand a few pumps before nudging me with his elbow. "My boy is being modest. He's getting promoted this week from sergeant to lieutenant and is on track to be the youngest police chief in the town's history."

"All right, enough." I should probably appreciate my dad's boasting on my behalf, but Bree isn't exactly falling over herself with cop worship. "This is Joan Sampson, president of the Deschutes Children's Welfare Society. A pillar of the community."

Mrs. Sampson beams and holds out her hand. "Also a retired teacher," she says, clutching Bree's hand in a grandmotherly grasp that almost makes me wonder if I imagined her badgering me to get naked. "It's lovely to meet you."

"You, too, ma'am." Bree's posture is perfect, and her manners suggest some fancy East Coast finishing school. Or maybe I read that in the paper, back when they profiled the family behind the development of Ponderosa Resort. "I'm so honored to have you with us."

"This place is incredible," I say, relieved we've moved past the subject of my career. "It's my first time making it out here."

"Thank you." Bree smiles wider, those lush lips parting just a little. I wonder if I'm the only one who just felt all the air leave his lungs. "My brothers and I have been working nonstop on the place since our father passed away eighteen months ago," she says. "We think he'd be proud of how we've transformed it."

"Your father was Cort Bracelyn." My father nods. "Helluva guy."

Is it my imagination, or did Bree's smile just wobble? But she rallies, pushing up the corners of her mouth to keep her expression cheerful. "Right," she says. "Yes. My father was—He didn't spend that much time out here."

My own father doesn't take the hint that maybe Bree would prefer not to make small talk about her dead dad. "He might not have been a regular resident, but he paid good wages to the guys running the ranch," he says. "We had a little dustup out here maybe eight years ago when some of his horses got loose and trampled a neighbor's fence. Your daddy was quick to pay retribution."

Bree's smile is tight. "He was always very generous with his money."

I don't know why, but I'm filled with a powerful urge to rescue her. To redirect this conversation I'm pretty sure she'd rather not have. "How are you liking Central Oregon?" I ask.

I sound like a lame caricature of a cop on a children's program, but Bree turns to me with thinly-disguised relief. "I love it out here," she says. "The people are so friendly, and I love seeing all the stars at night. And the coyotes—I hear them howling every night when I'm in bed."

My brain veers dangerously at the thought of Bree lying in bed with a thin sheet tracing the contours of those delectable curves, but I manage to hold it together. "I've always loved coyote singing, too," I admit. "That, and rain on a metal roof."

"I've hardly ever seen it rain out here," she says.

"That's why it's great. There's nothing like the smell of rain in the high desert. Ozone and sage and that herbal smell of wet juniper. Some of my favorite things in the world."

Her eyes hold mine, and I can tell she's imagining it. The patter of raindrops on the roof, the cinnamon scent of damp ponderosa bark, the rumble of thunder over the hills, my fingers in her hair as I tip her head back and—

"Austin has a pet coyote." My dad nudges me with his elbow, jarring me out of my fantasy.

Bree blinks. "A pet coyote?"

"She's a hybrid, actually," I say. "A coydog."

Bree tilts her head to look at me. "They're legal to have as pets?"

"Yes," I say a little too sharply. "I researched the hell out of the laws after I found her wandering in the Oregon Outback. The county regulations are looser than what I'd have to follow if I lived in the city limits."

My father laughs and claps me on the shoulder. "Austin's a stickler for the rules. Speaking of which…" He leans in close like he's got a big secret, and Bree's breast brushes my arm as she leans across me to hear him. It takes every ounce of strength I have to step back and break contact.

"With wildfire season still going strong, there's a ban on all open fires right now for public and private lands," he says. "We can let it slide since the ban gets lifted next week and you seem to have everything under control, but I thought you should know."

"Oh." Bree's cheeks go pink as she straightens up and looks my father in the eye. "I'm so sorry, I had no idea—we can put out the fire pits right now."

"Now don't you go worrying about it," he says with his *aw-shucks* smile. "Outside of town like this, and with all those fire extinguishers you've got lined up, we can make an exception. Besides, this hasn't been a bad fire year. It's really more of a suggestion than anything."

But Bree shakes her head, looking around like she expects a pair of deputies to dart out from behind the gazebo and slap the cuffs on her. "We want to follow the law out here." She looks at me when she says this, and I could swear she stands up a little straighter. "I believe in doing everything by the book. The laws exist for a reason, and I'm not one to break them."

Is it wrong that whole speech kinda turned me on?

But for some reason, I get the sense she's putting on an act. Most folks lace up their goody two shoes when they talk to cops, but hers don't fit quite right. There's something *off* in those pretty green eyes.

Bree clears her throat and looks back at my dad. "I should get back to the party," she says. "But don't worry; I'll have one of my brothers put the fires out right away."

"It's really not necessary," my father says. "But if it'll make you feel better—"

"It will." She smiles and takes a step back. "I always feel better when I'm doing the right thing."

She keeps edging away, like she's not quite ready to turn her back on us. When she finally does, I'm distracted by the wind flipping the hem of her dress, but I can't help noticing how she darts across the lawn like her feet caught fire.

I watch her go, admiring her curves, the fiery glint of sunlight in her dark curls, the daintiness of her calves, and I think I'd give anything to know what the hell makes Bree Bracelyn tick.

CHAPTER 2

BREE

*E*ven after I get the fire pits extinguished, there's a burning in my belly that won't die down. It flares up every time I drift close to Sergeant Sexypants, but maybe I'm imagining things.

And yes, I know what his dad said about the sergeant-to-lieutenant promotion and that he's even in line to be chief. That's worse, right? Bottom line, a cop is a cop is a cop, which is to say I'm staying the hell away from Officer McHottie.

"Hey, Bree—great party!"

I turn to Jade and Amber King, the sisters who own the reindeer ranch slash wedding venue next door. They're also boffing my cousin and brother, respectively, and I adore them both.

"I'm so glad you could make it." I pull Jade into a hug first, then Amber, and wonder for the umpteenth time what it would be like to have a sister instead of a gazillion half-brothers. Not that I'm complaining. Our father had many shortcomings like fidelity and marital success and—well, fatherhood. But he also had a talent for producing an abundance of smart, hardworking men with whom I share a business and a bloodline, so I can't fault the guy for that.

"Have you seen Sean?" I ask Amber.

That's my brother, the Michelin-starred chef who runs Juniper Fine Dining here at the resort. He's also head over heels in love with Amber, which is why she lights up like a Christmas tree when I say his name.

"He's running around like a crazy man in the kitchen," she says. "I told him to text me if he needs help with cleanup."

"We have staff for that." I cringe at the spoiled-rich-girl ring to my words, but Jade and Amber don't seem to notice. "Just have fun and enjoy yourselves," I tell them. "Did you get to tour the spa yet? Free chair massages."

"We were heading there next," Jade says. "We just finished the tour of the golf course. Brandon seems to think the golf carts are for speed racing."

As though summoned by his name, my cousin appears at his fiancée's side looking like a lovestruck teenager. He slides an arm around Jade's waist and plants a kiss on her temple, making her whole face flush pink before he looks at me. "Hey, Bree. You feeling good about the turnout?"

"It's terrific." I let my gaze sweep over the crowd, noticing city council members and business owners, the mayor, and even a senator. My gaze snags on the hot cop, and since he's not looking up at this hill where I'm standing, I let myself linger. He has broad shoulders and ramrod-straight posture, but there's something in his smile that's calming. Normally, cops make my pulse pound. So does he, but for different reasons. His dad says something to him and he laughs, and I try to recall the difference between the police and the sheriff.

"What's with all the cops out here?" I ask. "I met the sheriff, and also his son who's with police department. I'm not sure I know the difference."

I look back in time to see Jade and Amber exchange a private smile, and I'm sure they just saw me checking out Austin. Thankfully, they're too classy to say anything. "The police deal with crimes in the city limits," Jade explains. "And the sheriff's department deals with stuff outside the city."

"There's some overlap, though," Amber adds. "Especially since we're close to the edge of town. But mostly the sheriff's department is our go-to crime fighting squad out here."

I don't know if I'm relieved or disappointed that Austin won't be coming to my rescue if I call 911 to report my panties caught fire. Not that I'd do that. I'm just saying, Tasty Cop is *not* going to be my savior.

I try to think of something I can ask about him, but the questions take absurd forms in my head.

How well do you know Chief Studly?

Is he married or divorced or single?

Is he looking for someone to share his bed and have his babies and—

"Knock it off." I don't mean to say the words out loud, but somehow I do. The sisters exchange a look again before Jade turns and looks up at Brandon.

"Wasn't Austin in your grade?" she asks him.

"Yeah." Brandon waves to someone, and I realize with a jolt that it's Austin. He returns Brandon's wave, then starts toward us, and my heart does a big ol' cannonball into my stomach.

"We played football together," Brandon says as Austin draws closer. "Good guy."

"Single, too," Amber adds. "Never married."

She might be my favorite sister.

"Everyone says he's a shoo-in to make chief next year when Fred Maxwell retires," Jade says, moving back up the favorite-sister rankings with her addition to my arsenal of information. "He's one of the few guys on the force with a master's degree, plus he's always going to these FBI leadership training things."

"Ambitious guy," I say mildly as I try not to stare.

"The dude works his ass off," Brandon says as Austin saunters up beside us and slaps his hand against Brandon's.

"Hey, man."

They exchange one of those complicated bro handshakes, which gives me ten seconds to check him out. He's even hotter than I remember, all dark hair and burly cop muscles and clear gray-blue eyes that I could swear looked right through me when we met earlier.

That's downright terrifying, and so is the way I'm responding to him like a moony-eyed middle schooler. I've never been turned on by a man in uniform, so why am I checking him out like he's lava cake on a dessert cart?

"Ladies." Austin nods to Jade and Amber before his eyes land on me. I don't know why, but I stand up straighter, struggling to pretend I didn't just do one of those weird full-body shivers.

"Bree, right?" He smiles and *ohmylord* it takes everything I've got not to melt into a puddle at his feet.

"That's right," I say, already forgetting the question. My name? Hell, that's anyone's guess right now. I'm so tongue-tied I can hardly recall the alphabet, which is so not like me. I'm usually pretty adept at the social thing.

I clear my throat and order myself to stop acting like an idiot. "What's the Oregon Outback?"

He gives me a quizzical look then snaps his fingers. "That's right, I forgot I told you where I found Virginia."

"Your dog's name is Virginia?"

"Yep." He smiles, crinkling the edges of those blue-gray eyes. "Virginia Woof."

It takes me a second to get it. "As in Virginia *Woolf*?" He nods, and it's a struggle to keep my face from registering shock. "You named your dog after the foremost modernist author of the twentieth century? The pioneer of narrative device and stream of consciousness prose?"

He quirks an eyebrow at me. "Can't say much about my dog's writing," he says. "I found her wallowing around in the bed of Lake Abert. It's the only saltwater lake in Oregon, but it's been drying up."

"Lousy deal for all the brine shrimp fishermen," Brandon puts in. "Not to mention migratory birds."

"Right, that's the hell of it," Austin says. "Anyway, she was scrawny and full of parasites, and she had all these pebbles wedged so deep in her paw pads that they'd started to grow over. It was like things got so bad that she filled her pockets with rocks and tried to drown herself in the damn lake—"

"Like Virginia Woolf." I get it now.

"Exactly," he says. "Only there wasn't enough water to do the job."

"So you saved her." My chest floods with new respect for Officer Yummylicious.

He gives a modest shrug. "She's doing great now," he says. "Anyway, that whole area out there is part of the Oregon Outback."

"Where is it?"

"South-Central Oregon as you're heading toward California," he says. "It's pretty remote. Mostly dirt roads and rattlesnakes, but there's also some cool stuff like Fort Rock and Summer Lake Hot Springs."

"A real hot springs?" That sounds dumb, but I've never seen one.

Austin nods, and there's that smile again. "It's rustic, but beautiful. I'd be glad to show it to you sometime."

I stare at him for a few beats, not sure if he's just asked me out or if he's playing friendly-neighborhood cop. I don't want to be presumptuous. "How far is it?"

"Couple hours, give or take. It's a long day trip or a good overnight. Not that I was suggesting an overnight date."

"Date," I repeat, grateful at least that he put it out there. "As in —*date*-date?"

Jesus, Bree, you sound like an idiot.

Austin grins and shoves his hands in his pockets. "Yeah, I was thinking date, but a *date*-date works, too. The quantity is up to you."

Good Lord, he's flirting, and it might be the most charming thing I've ever seen. But I really need to nip this in the bud.

"That's really sweet, but I actually don't date cops."

The second the words leave my mouth, I realize how ridiculous they sound. Jade and Amber shoot me matching incredulous looks, and I wish I could rewind the tape and stick with, "I'm too focused on work to date anyone."

Austin, bless his heart, is doing his best not to stare at me as though I've announced a fondness for liverwurst pancakes. "This is like—an unwavering personal policy?"

"Right," I say, figuring I might as well go with it. "It's just a personality thing, I guess."

Those blue-gray eyes bore into mine, looking more bemused than offended. "No problem," he says. "I'll hand in my resignation tomorrow."

He's stone-faced, so it takes me a second to catch the glint in his eye. I bust out laughing, I can't help it. "You'll quit being a cop?"

"Sure, if that's what it takes." He scuffs a toe in the dirt. "Shouldn't take them more than a few weeks to find my replacement, and then I'll take you out for dinner at that cool Portuguese place downtown."

"Sintra," Brandon offers. "Great linguica tacos."

"Sure, we'll have that." Austin smiles, and I hear Amber giggle beside me.

My heart does a cartwheel, but I keep my expression neutral and fold my arms over my chest. "How do you plan to pay for this date if you're jobless all of a sudden?"

"No problem, I'll get a new job." He looks thoughtful. "I'm thinking shepherd."

"Shepherd?"

"Sure, I like sheep," he says. "Or maybe an astronaut. You think NASA's hiring?"

"Maybe, but you'd have to move to DC or Houston," I point out, trying not to flirt. This isn't flirting, right? "Being that far away is going to make dating difficult."

"Good point." He pretends to think. "I suppose I could be a snake milker."

I give a super-uncool snort-laugh. "For all that snake milk they're selling in grocery stores?"

Amber laughs again, but Jade looks thoughtful. "That's actually a real job, isn't it? I saw it on TV."

"Yep," Austin confirms. "They're zoologists who extract venom from snakes for medical research."

"Is that how they make antivenom?" Amber asks.

"Yeah." He's answering Amber, but his eyes are fixed on me. "It's a noble career, and I'm guessing you've never dated a snake milker."

"I'm guessing I don't want to." Truth be told, I'm rethinking my policy on the cop thing.

Austin brings his hand to his chin and pretends to ponder some more. "Harsh. Okay, how about if I become a chicken sexer?"

"A chicken sexer?" I can't stifle the laughter, but I stop and consider whether this might be a real job, too. "Wait, is that someone who determines the sex of chickens?"

"Bingo."

He grins as Brandon does an imitation of a startled chicken. Cluck-cluck-cluck-*squawk*!

"They work for commercial hatcheries where they've gotta figure out right away what gender the chicks are." Austin slugs Brandon in the shoulder to make him quit the chicken impression. "I hear it's pretty lucrative, so I'll be able to take us out to some nice places."

This is hands-down the most bizarre flirtation I've ever been party to, but I can't stop smiling. Can't stop feeling like I've got a cinnamon jawbreaker in the center of my belly. "How do you expect me to tell my friends and family I'm dating a chicken sexer?" I ask.

"You've got me there." He drums his fingers together in mock contemplation, then snaps. "Got it. How about an iceberg mover?"

"That's a thing?"

"Sure it is." He grins. "They track where the icebergs are at and then tell the shipping companies how to get around them. Sometimes they even hook them up with cables and drag them away."

"Don't you have to be with the Coast Guard to do that?" Amber asks.

"Good point," Austin says. "I suppose I'll have to enlist. Do you have a problem with all men in uniform or just cops?"

The hair on my arms prickles, and I feel my smile stiffen. That's right, we were talking about cops. Cops and why I don't date them.

As much as I'm loving flirting with Austin, I've gotta be straight with him. "You seem like a great guy, you really do, but—"

"But you can't ask me to give up my career for you?" He nods, not looking particularly hurt. "Fair enough. I suppose we did just meet."

"Right," I say, though there's something about Austin that makes me feel like I've known him a while. I might not be into cops, but there's something about this one that grabs me.

All the more reason to keep your distance.

I take a deep breath and don my best public relations mask. "It's been really great meeting you, though," I tell him. "I'm sure I'll see you around."

"I'm sure you will." He gives me a mini-salute, and those blue-gray eyes hold mine for a few more breaths. "If you change your mind about dating a cop-turned-shepherd-turned-astronaut-turned-snake milker-turned-chicken sexer-turned iceberg mover, you know where to find me."

He turns and saunters down the hill, taking an unexpected hunk of my heart with him.

CHAPTER 3

AUSTIN

I know I should keep my distance from Bree Bracelyn. She made it clear she doesn't date cops, and I can respect that. But somehow, I find myself driving to her house the Monday after the party, a tiny fork shoved in the breast pocket of my uniform.

It's not as weird as it sounds. Okay, it's a little weird. I'm returning the shrimp fork my father "borrowed." To his credit, he didn't mean to steal the damn thing. He's constantly tucking things in his pockets—pens from checkout counters, gloves that look like his—and discovering later he's an accidental thief.

Why do I have a hunch it's not accidental this time?

"Do me a favor and take this back to the resort," he asked me this morning when we met for a pre-shift breakfast at the Dandelion Café.

I studied him over the rim of my coffee mug, looking for signs of scheming. There were none, which isn't surprising. You don't become sheriff without a damn good poker face. "Why me?"

"Because you live close." My dad grinned and picked up his own coffee mug. "And because you didn't stop staring at that pretty brunette all night."

I would have argued, but he's right. Ponderosa Resort is on my way home, and yeah, I thought about Bree all weekend.

I'm still thinking about her as I wind my way up the driveway to the main lodge, the windows of my squad car cracked to let the juniper-spiked breeze swirl through. Towering aspens line the road, half of them quivering with gold-tipped leaves. Fall has been unseasonably warm so far, but cool weather isn't far off. Maybe Bree needs someone to rake her leaves.

That wasn't a euphemism, but yeah, fine. I want to see Bree. Is that so wrong? Maybe I can't date her, but I can make her laugh, make her toss those glossy curls that leave me wondering what it would feel like to twist my fingers up in all that chocolaty warmth. God, those green eyes. And that mouth. And—

I shake myself out of it as I pull up in front of the main lodge. Standing off to one side is a guy the size of an NFL lineman. He's wearing a Ponderosa Ranch T-shirt and work gloves covered in tree sap. The scruffy beard doesn't cover the scowl that looks like a permanent fixture, and I wonder if he's one of Bree's brothers. If so, he's not one I met the other day.

The guy looks up as I approach, but he doesn't smile or look surprised. Just stares like a grumpy lumberjack whose tree just fell on a car.

"Evening," I say by way of greeting. "Any idea where I can find Bree Bracelyn?"

He studies me without blinking. "Yep," he says. "You're Lieutenant Dugan?"

I glance down and see I'm still wearing the badge that says *Sergeant*. The promotion isn't official for a couple days, and I'm a stickler for the rules, so the gold bar and Lieutenant badge are still in my desk. Does that mean Bree's been talking about me?

The big guy kills that hope in a hurry. "Saw your picture in the paper when they announced the promotion," he says. "And your name was in there this morning, too. Something about an old case getting reopened."

"The Zonski case," I say automatically as my gut coils into a knot. "Homicide."

"Yeah. That was it."

He stares at me some more, and I realize I still don't know who the hell he is. The way he's watching me suggests a decision in progress—to grant access to Bree or to chase me off the property with a shotgun. I don't see one lying around, but maybe I should have worn Kevlar.

The guy seems to decide something then. "Mark Bracelyn. Bree's brother." He doesn't extend a hand, but does reach into his pocket and pull out a phone. "Let me check on her."

He turns his back to me and starts punching numbers. I hear it ring once, twice, and then a muffled version of Bree's voice.

"Cop's here," he says instead of hello. "You want to see him or not?"

There's a long stretch of silence, and I wonder whether Mark turned down the volume, or if Bree really has nothing to say. I'm on the brink of just handing the damn fork to Mark and calling it a day when I hear Bree's muffled voice.

"I'll be right there," she says. "Have him wait in my office."

Mark clicks off the phone and looks at me, then nods toward the lodge. "Head in through those doors and take a left," he says. "She'll be over in a minute."

"Thank you."

"Restaurant's closed now, but there's coffee in the lobby. Don't break anything, and don't touch anything in Bree's office."

I'm getting the sense this brother isn't the chief of hospitality, but at least he's not running me off the property. "Thanks."

"Sure."

He turns back to a massive pile of lumber and grabs an axe I'm glad I didn't notice before. The guy doesn't seem violent, but he's definitely got some issues.

I turn and make my way toward a pair of double doors that

must be fifteen feet tall. The building is massive, constructed to look like an old cedar barn, but with huge banks of windows and a fancy-looking fountain at the head of the paver-stone walkway.

The doors swish open as I approach, making me feel like some kind of royalty. The entryway is done in weathered slate and rustic-looking barn wood, and there's an enormous hammered copper bar in the restaurant off to my right.

I hang a left like Mark told me, heeding the warning not to break anything. Not that I'm in the habit of smashing vases of dried cornflowers in the foyers of luxury lodges, but I shove my hands in my pockets anyway. The space smells like warm cedar and fresh sage, and I wonder if it's natural or some high-tech air freshener. The artwork is sparse but mostly tasteful-looking Native American pieces that might be the real deal. There was something in the paper last month about the Ponderosa Resort folks working closely with the Warm Springs tribe to honor local culture and heritage, and I wonder if that's Bree's doing.

I glance at the reception desk that's unmanned at the moment. Signs crafted with cast iron and copper point the way to the restaurant, the lodge rooms, and the Desert Lily Float Center. I'm wondering what the hell that is when Bree walks through the door.

"Austin."

Her voice is breathless, which makes two of us. Damned if she doesn't take my breath away. She's wearing a tight black skirt with a shiny-looking gray blouse tucked into it, and her cheeks are flushed. "Please, come in."

She gestures toward her office, and I follow, inhaling the scent of expensive perfume. Not that I know what expensive perfume smells like, but it's flowery and delicate with a hint of something like oak-moss. I order myself not to stare at her ass as she rounds the corner of a sleek walnut desk that's bare except for a fancy-looking laptop and a chrome pen holder. I lower myself into the leather chair on the opposite side of the desk, grateful there's a piece of furniture between us. That'll keep me from staring at her legs.

Bree folds her hands on the desk and licks her lips, which gets me staring at her mouth again. She's wearing some kind of glossy lip stuff, and I wonder if it tastes like raspberries.

It takes me a second to remember why I'm here. "I came to give you a fork."

Bree blinks. "Pardon me?"

I fumble into my pocket, hurrying to produce the small silver utensil. "I think it's yours," I say, holding out a flattened palm to offer it to her. "My dad walked off with it by accident. Figured I'd bring it by since I live just down the road."

"Oh. Thank you." Bree hesitates, then reaches out to take it. Her fingertips brush the center of my palm, lingering longer than required for such a simple task, but I don't dare break contact. I don't dare breathe. Her hand feels warm and delicate, and I'm not sure what's happening here.

Bree gives me a shy smile and draws her hand back. She curls her fingers around the fork but makes no move to usher me out. "You live close?"

"On a couple acres just south of here. Log cabin with a red roof?"

Surprise flickers in her green eyes. "Oh. I've seen that place. The one with the big front porch?"

"Yes, ma'am."

She smiles and threads her fingers through her hair, or at least tries to. She seems to forget the fork, and the tiny utensil winds up tangled in her curls.

"Ow. Shit." She yanks at it, and I worry she's going to pull out a hunk of scalp.

"Let me." I stretch across the desk to untangle her, careful not to tug too hard. Her hair is even softer than I expected, and I order myself to hurry up and stop fondling her curls. "Got it."

I draw back and hand over the fork again. "Here you go."

"Thanks." She gives a nervous little laugh and plucks it from my palm a little quicker this time. "Sorry, I'm a little out of it. I've got this crazy FAM trip running right now, and it's nonstop with these guys."

"FAM trip?"

"Familiarization tour." She sets down the fork and picks up a pen, though it doesn't look like she plans to write anything. Just turns it over in her fingers as she speaks. "It's PR-speak for bringing in a bunch of influential journalists and bloggers and giving them the royal treatment."

"You guys aren't open to regular guests yet, right?"

"The restaurant is, but not the lodging side," she says, still flipping the pen. "I wanted to get a couple FAM groups through first to make sure they have the best experience possible."

"And then they write about it," I say, earning a nod from Bree. "Or post on Instagram or Facebook or whatever travel journalists do these days."

"Exactly," Bree says. "I've got a mix here at the moment—some traditional print media, some digital influencers. One of them's actually my best friend from college here with his husband. They have this super-popular travel blog called Nomadic Dudes with more than eight-hundred-thousand page views a month. They're normally booked out years in advance, but I got lucky and lured them here on short notice."

"That's great," I say. "Congratulations."

She watches my face like she's expecting more. A reaction of some kind, maybe a homophobic remark or some condescending quip about nepotism or social media.

Not my style. Not even close. "So you manage all of that?" I ask. "The FAM tours and the marketing and stuff?"

She nods, her expression softening ever so slightly. "I have a marketing assistant, but I'm pretty hands-on with these first few trips."

"Sounds like a lot of work."

She tilts her head to the side like she hadn't considered that. "I suppose so. I don't really mind." A funny little smile crosses her face, and she stops flipping the pen. "I guess I've sort of trained for the happy hostess role my whole life."

"You have a marketing degree from Purdue, plus an MBA from Northwestern."

The pen drops from her fingers, and she fumbles to grab it again. "Oh. Yes. I—did you look that up in some kind of police database or something?"

I laugh, which I probably shouldn't. She seems flustered. "Nothing that high-tech. It's on your website."

"Oh. Duh." Her face reddens, and she glances down at her hands. "Right, I forgot about the bio page."

And I forgot that I only looked at Bree's section and totally skipped the brothers. I hope there's no quiz later.

I definitely checked out Bree, though. Born in Connecticut, she went to some elite boarding school in Rhode Island before heading off to college. Loves fine wine, art history, and dogs—the latter evidenced by a photo of her frolicking with a trio of pups from the Humane Society when they christened the new dog park here at the resort.

Gotta admit, my dog-loving heart sat up and panted when I watched the YouTube video of her passing a check for ten grand to the folks at the animal shelter. I love the altruism, sure, but not as much as I loved seeing Bree in blue jeans with wind-tousled curls talking about how she wants a dog of her own once she's settled in.

Would it be wrong to woo her with mine?

I order myself to stop being a dick and stick with the conversation at hand. "What did you mean by that?" I ask. "About training for the happy hostess thing your whole life?"

Her smile is guarded, and I wonder if she didn't intend to use those words. It wouldn't be the first time someone's confessed something they didn't mean to tell me. It's a fringe benefit of the cop thing.

"I guess I meant my mom," she says slowly. "She's one of those society ladies who's always hosting elaborate events and charity balls. I learned to throw an eight-course dinner party in grade school."

"Seriously?"

She smiles, but there's an odd wistfulness to it. "I was the only twelve-year-old with her own collection of Robbe & Berking French Pearl flatware to serve three dozen. Suffice it to say, I was an awkward middle schooler."

A flicker of sadness lights her eyes, but it's gone fast. I feel an urge to fill the silence, to keep us from stumbling over something dark and melancholy. "I think it sounds pretty impressive," I tell her, not sure what the hell Robbe & Berking French whatever means. "My mom coached me for days about which fork to use on prom night, and I still screwed it up."

"Prom night." She says the words like they're a foreign language. "I always wanted one of those."

"You didn't go to prom?"

"We didn't have a prom." She folds her hands on the desk, and there's that wistful look again. "I went to an all-girls' prep school. The closest we came was when we'd have formal dances with the boys' school nearby, but I didn't go to those, either."

"Too busy hosting dinner parties?" I'm aiming for lighthearted teasing, but it's clear I missed the mark. Her green eyes flicker, and she looks down at her hands again.

"I wasn't exactly the most popular girl in school."

Damn. Why the hell did I say that?

"If it makes you feel better," I offer, "I got a lot of shit from guys in high school. When your dad's a cop, you're the last guy people want at their keg parties."

She looks up, those green eyes assessing. "Were you bullied?"

I shake my head, almost ashamed to admit that's not my story. Was it hers? "I was never the big man on campus like Brandon Brown, but I got along with everyone. Lettered in three sports, went to all the dances, that sort of thing."

I shut my mouth, hoping I don't sound like some douchebag who's stuck wallowing in his glory days as a teenage letterman. Bree looks at me strangely, but I can't read her expression.

"Were your parents—" She stops there and shakes her head. "Sorry, I'm not trying to be nosy."

"Nose away." I get the sense it freaks her out when I'm the one asking questions, like it's cop interrogation mode or something. If it keeps her talking, I'd cheerfully sit here all day letting her quiz me on my favorite yogurt flavor or what size boxer briefs I wear.

But she asked about my family. "My parents have been married thirty-five years," I tell her. "Very happily. And I have three sisters."

Bree laughs and rolls the pen between her palms. "That's a lot of estrogen in one house." She shakes her head. "I pretty much grew up an only child."

She must notice the surprise on my face because she hurries to explain. "My brothers and I have different mothers. Same dad, but different moms."

"Ah," I say, struggling to wrap my brain around that. "So you and Mark don't have the same mother?"

She laughs and shakes her head. "No. My dad actually left my mom for Mark's mom, which was only fair since *my* mom stole him from Sean's mom, who stole him from James's mom, and— well, anyway. You don't need the whole sordid tale. Long story short, Dad got around."

Holy crap. And I thought my family had issues.

"Sean is the chef," I say, remembering him from the event the other night. "What does Mark do?"

"Vice President of Grounds Management, but he hates that title," she says. "And James was a lawyer, and he's technically the CEO, but we all have the same ownership. And I guess Johnathan isn't here, so—"

"Wait, how many brothers do you have?"

She presses her lips together. "A lot."

"And you didn't grow up together?"

"Nope." She makes a face, but at least now she doesn't look uncomfortable. Not like she did a few minutes ago. "I might see a brother or two when our visits with Dad overlapped, but mostly we were raised separately."

"You seem pretty tight now," I observe, thinking about the protective look on Mark's face. "I suppose you'd have to get along well, running a business together."

"Our dad dying brought us closer, I guess. How's that for dysfunctional?"

I'm not sure how to answer, so I settle for making a noncommittal grunt-hum as I try to recall if I ever met her father. I remember a photo in the paper of a tall guy in a pressed shirt shaking hands with the mayor. He made a huge donation to some local charity, and there'd been talk of a run for political office before he died.

"Your dad owned the ranch for a long time?"

"Yeah, but he wasn't here much," she says. "He bought and sold property like baseball cards, but this one he hung on to. He came out here a few times a year to play cowboy."

"I don't remember seeing you around." And I definitely would have remembered her. Those green eyes alone would have burned themselves into my memory.

"My schooling kept me away a lot." She looks down at her hands, and there's that discomfort again. It's pretty clear Bree doesn't like talking about her childhood. Her dysfunctional family, sure, but not herself.

When she looks up, she's got her PR professional mask back in place. "Did you always want to be a cop?"

"Yeah," I admit. "Always. My dad and I are pretty tight. I never considered any career besides law enforcement."

She smiles, and there's a warmth in her eyes again. We're back on safe ground. "You mean besides chicken sexing or iceberg moving?"

I laugh. "Besides that." There's a question I've been wanting to ask her, but I've probably exceeded my limit. Still, I can't shake the urge to know. "Did you have a bad experience dating a cop or something?"

Her mask falters, but Bree does a good job shoving it back into place. She picks up her pen again like it's a magic wand, and she's poised to wave away the uncomfortable subject. "No," she says, but there's hesitation. "It's just a personality thing."

I wait for her to elaborate, to say more about why we won't be going out for dinner and getting married and having babies and —wait, why am I thinking like this?

"So you're with the police department, but your dad is the sheriff," she says, clearing her throat along with our conversational slate. "How'd that happen?"

"Guess I wanted to forge my own path," I admit. "To get out of his shadow and make my own place in the world."

"That's very noble."

"I'm a noble kinda guy," I tease. "My sisters used to joke that I have a lousy sense of direction because my brain's entire navigational system is made up of moral compass. Prince Goody Two-Shoes, they called me."

I'm trying for lighthearted joking, and again, I fail. There's that flicker in Bree's eyes, and I can't figure out how I keep missing the mark with this woman. I'm a people person, dammit. Total strangers confess things to me, and I can make the surliest asshole smile.

Maybe not Bree's brother, but *most* people.

She sits there in silence, rubbing her lips together, and I catch myself thinking about raspberries again. Is her mouth as soft as it looks? What would it feel like to press my—

"Did you want something?"

I jerk my gaze off her mouth and back to her eyes. *Busted.* At least I wasn't staring at her breasts. "I'm sorry?"

"To drink." Bree smiles, and I can't tell if she knows I was thinking about kissing her, or if she's being polite. "Sean makes this great cucumber-infused water with fresh mint and lemon. It's really refreshing. Or there's soda or beer or wine or—wait, no." She drops the pen again, and it rolls to the edge of the desk. "You're in uniform, and you're driving, so obviously I'm not offering alcohol."

I laugh and lean back in my seat. "I'd love some of that water. I wouldn't mind checking out the restaurant, actually."

"You didn't get the tour the other night?"

"Nope. I saw the golf course and the ballroom and the event center, but I got tied up talking to people and missed the rest of it."

Bree stands up and rounds the desk. "I'd love for you to see it. Come on."

I stand and follow her back through the lobby. Her hips sway as she rounds a rustic-looking sign that spells out "Juniper Fine Dining" in weathered copper letters.

"I really like the way you guys decorated," I offer, determined to admire the décor instead of her ass.

"Thanks." She stops beside the hammered copper bar and smiles. "We were going for rustic Northwest with a touch of luxury."

"I didn't know that was a thing, but you nailed it." I run a palm over one of the live-edge juniper tabletops. "These are amazing."

Bree doesn't respond, and I glance up to see her staring at my hand. Her throat moves as she swallows, and she gives a funny little laugh. "Sorry, I—I don't think I've ever seen anyone with such big hands. I noticed earlier with the fork and um—"

I lift the right one and give a magician-like swoop. "Makes it tough to find gloves that fit, but I could palm a basketball from the time I was twelve."

There I go sounding like a dumbshit jock again. Bree stares at my hand for a few more beats, and I wish I could stop thinking about running my palm down the curve of her back.

She clears her throat. "Right, well, my brothers and Brandon made all the tables. And we built this space so every table has a view of the Cascade Mountains. Lots of high desert eye candy to go around."

I glance out the window, rewarded by breathtaking views of South, Middle, and North Sister laid out like snow-capped gems on green felt. "I'll bet the sunsets are killer."

She nods. "Our sunset dinner hours have already booked up months in advance, and we've been scheduling weddings pretty steadily."

"I'm not surprised," I say. "The place is great. The food the other night was amazing."

"That's all Sean," she says. "He makes this salt-cured lamb that's positively mouthwatering."

My eyes drop to her mouth again; I can't help it. As my heart stutters, I force myself to look away, to study anything in this bar but Bree Bracelyn's beautiful mouth. A glass water dispenser sits on one end of the bar, half full and shimmering with ice cubes and flecks of mint and thin cucumber slices. It looks icy and cool, and I'm suddenly thirsty as hell.

Or maybe Bree's doing that to me. I can feel her watching, assessing me for something. What?

"I haven't," she says softly.

I meet her eyes again, confused.

"Dated a cop," she answers, circling back to the question I asked in her office. "Ever."

She takes a step closer and looks up, green eyes searching mine. I drop my gaze to her mouth, surprised to find it scant inches from mine. I think about raspberries again, about how goddamn much I want to kiss her. I force myself to meet her eyes as I shove my hands in my pockets, not sure what's happening.

She reads my mind again. "I've never kissed a cop, either."

My brain is two steps behind and scrambling to catch up when her lips touch mine. They're tentative at first, testing me. Waiting to see how I'll respond.

And I do respond, slowly at first. Her mouth is soft and willing and *oh my God* she does taste like raspberries. Raspberries and mint, even though she hasn't sipped the water.

I drink her in, pulling her tight against me to deepen the kiss. Bree presses her whole body against me and gives a soft little sigh. My hands press into the small of her back as she kisses me with a hunger that goes beyond a simple taste test.

Hands rake down my back, fingernails staking their claim. I lean back against a table, trying to even out our height difference. I'm at least a foot taller than her, but she steps into the space between my splayed legs and everything lines up perfectly.

I still can't believe this is happening, but I don't stop. I couldn't stop if my life depended on it, so I hope it doesn't. I slide my fingers into those dark curls, something I've been aching to do since we met. They're silky and thick, and I tunnel in deep. *Soft.* She's soft everywhere, so soft I could drown in her.

She presses closer, nudging the arousal between my legs. Is this some kind of test? I don't know if I'm failing or passing, but Christ, she feels good. My brain spins with questions, but the rest of me doesn't give a damn about answers. All I want is Bree, the lush warmth of her body against mine, the smell of flowers and raspberries and—

"Excuse me?"

I jerk at the voice behind me. It's followed by a raspy throat clearing, and Bree jumps back so fast she trips over my foot. I reach out to steady her and turn to face the door.

A twenty-something guy stands at the other end of the bar wearing glasses and a frantic expression. His eyes shift from Bree to me, then widen with surprise.

"Thank God you're here," he says. "I need to report a crime."

CHAPTER 4

"*I need to report a crime.*"

Six words no PR professional wants to hear on day one of a FAM tour that includes some of the biggest bloggers and travel writers in the industry.

One of those writers is standing next to my bar looking at me like I'm some kind of brazen hussy. Which I kind of am, since I totally jumped Captain Tastycakes after telling myself—and him—I wasn't interested. What the hell is wrong with me?

But that's the least of my worries right now.

"What's the matter, Graham?" I use my most soothing public relations voice, hopeful we can avoid involving the cops. It doesn't help that there's a cop standing next to me with an impressive erection tenting the front of his uniform pants. I slip in front of Austin and hope to God that Graham hasn't noticed.

But Graham has other things on his mind that don't involve Hottie Cop's impressive hard-on.

"I ordered a pizza, right?" Graham slides a MacBook from the messenger bag that bisects his wiry frame. "I did it through your online portal, just like the instructions say."

I'm not sure whether to be relieved or annoyed that the

supposed crime involves pepperoni, but I nod and do my best to keep a straight face. "Yes, well, we're still working out the kinks in the system."

"No, that's not the crime," he scoffs. "The delivery driver pulled up outside my cabin, and Carl Montlake from the *Seattle Times* travel section went running out and took my goddamned pizza."

And the crime is felony cock blocking...

I bite back the words as I stare at him, trying to muster up the right amount of horror. "You're saying a Pulitzer-winning travel journalist stole your pizza."

"That's right." Graham has the wherewithal to look a little embarrassed at hearing the words aloud, but he doesn't lose the indignant posture. "Your marketing materials say Ponderosa guests can have any cuisine they want brought to their rooms in a snap, but what systems do you have in place to prevent theft?"

I start to point out that the resort's state-of-the-art security system is designed to prevent the theft of jewelry and cash, not Canadian bacon.

But that's when Austin speaks up. "Would you like me to check into it?"

I most assuredly would not like Austin Dugan snooping around my property or my life, but Graham the travel blogger is quick to take him up on it.

"I'd like to file a report," he says. "And I'd like you to talk to that entitled prick, Carl. This is not how a luxury resort should run."

All right, things are getting out of hand here. I grit my teeth while aiming my most cheerful smile at Graham. "May I take a look at your laptop?"

He clutches it to his chest like I've just asked to borrow his underwear. "Of course not! All my notes are on here. And my stories and—"

"Never mind, I'll use the restaurant's computer."

I round the copper-topped bar and snatch Sean's laptop from beside the cash register. Luckily, my brother's computer is not a bastion of security. It takes me two guesses to figure out his password is "Amber69," and before I know it, I'm logged in to the back end of the resort's delivery management system.

"Let's see," I say, scrolling through data on recent orders. "It looks like you ordered a large, gluten-free, dairy-free pizza with organic farm veggies at six-twenty-three p.m."

"That's right," Graham says, sounding vindicated already. "Gigi doesn't do dairy or gluten, and she's the one who wanted the pizza."

It doesn't surprise me that Graham's other half—Gigi Gresham, a waiflike Instagram darling who's forever posting photos of herself gazing pensively from balconies with quotes like "live your dreams" or "#blessed"—would be a picky eater. She's part of the power duo behind the uber-popular Lovebird Journeys travel blog, and the fact that Graham and Gigi have more than a quarter-million followers is why he's standing here right now.

"Let's see," I say, scrolling through the delivery management system. "It looks like Carl Montlake from the *Seattle Times* also ordered a pizza. His was the Summer Harvest pizza featuring an avocado cream base, roasted poblano, zucchini squash, smoked corn, and cherry tomato."

"Sounds tasty," Austin says.

"It does, doesn't it?" I turn back to Graham, whose face has fallen. "It's been very popular with the culinary crowd. It looks like *your* pizza should be here in about ten minutes."

Graham's face goes red. He frowns and lowers his laptop to his side. "I, uh—"

"Why don't you head back over to your cabin?" I close Sean's laptop and turn to the wine rack that occupies a full wall beside the bar. It doesn't take me long to find the bottle I'm after. "This is the 2013 Sangiovese from Lange Estate Winery over in

Dundee. It's the perfect pairing for the gluten-free, dairy-free, veggie pizza."

I smile and hold the bottle out to Graham like we're best pals. "Compliments of the house."

"Oh." He takes the bottle, and I watch the bluster leak out of him as he realizes he's not about to be chastised by me or the police. "That would be great." He straightens up and tugs at his shirt hem. "Thank you."

"My pleasure."

He shoves the bottle in his messenger bag, nods to Austin, and marches out of the restaurant with a lot less swagger than he entered with.

Not that I saw him enter. I might have been distracted by Austin's tongue in my mouth. I turn back to Hottie Cop as the heat creeps into my cheeks.

"Look, Austin—"

"That was amazing."

I lick my lips, determined not to get derailed by my desperate urge to kiss him again. "It was pretty great, but we really shouldn't have done it. I made this big deal about not dating cops, and then I go and throw myself at you like some kind of—"

"I was talking about how you handled Graham." Austin grins. "But you're right, the kiss was amazing, too."

If I thought my face couldn't get any hotter, I was wrong. My cheeks go positively nuclear under Austin's watchful gaze. "Right. Um—"

"Relax, Bree." He takes a step closer and tucks an escaped curl behind my ear. I do my best not to mount his leg like a Labrador in heat. "You've got a talent for handling people."

I must look embarrassed, because Austin hurries to clarify. "Still talking about Graham. The way you sent him out of here feeling like he won instead of like the dumbass he was?"

"Oh. Right." I clear my throat. "It's all part of the public relations thing."

"Well, you're good at it."

"Thank you. We're selling a pleasurable luxury experience here," I say, my voice catching a little on *pleasurable*. "It pays to keep our customers happy, even if they are being dumbasses."

"Very sneaky." He grins when he says it, and I can tell he's joking, but something uneasy unfurls in my belly.

"I guess I can relate," he says. "There's a certain level of manipulation that goes into good investigation work. You've gotta tread carefully if you want to get the confession."

A lead ball lands in my gut, and it's all I can do to keep my breath from coming out in a whoosh. I'm still smiling, but inside I feel like my guts are coming unraveled.

Good God, what was I thinking making out with a cop? With a guy whose freakin' job it is to uncover people's secrets? With a guy who's ambitious and moral and in line to be the next goddamn police chief?

I take a step back, doing my best to stop thinking about that kiss. About all the risks that come with it, both for him and for me. "Right. Well, I should probably get back to work."

It occurs to me that I never gave him a full tour or got him that damn cucumber water, and I half expect him to call me on it. But Austin just looks into my eyes. He stares for so long that I start to worry he's reading my thoughts.

Please don't do that.

"Sure," he says, straightening up. "I'd better get home to feed Virginia."

"Virginia." His dog, right. "Give her a scratch for me."

I step back again, wishing I didn't have to herd him out of here like a misbehaving guest.

Wishing, not for the first time, that I didn't have to keep my distance from Austin Dugan.

* * *

THREE DAYS LATER, I'm gathered with my siblings for a resort meeting. The journalists from the FAM group had breakfast an hour ago and set off for a day hike with our activities coordinator. Since the lunch rush won't hit for another couple hours, my brothers and I have commandeered a corner table with the best view of the mountains.

"Brunch is served." Sean sails out of the kitchen with a plate piled high with his famous breakfast burritos. They're filled with sage-spiced chicken sausage, organic eggs, smoked gouda, roasted sweet potatoes, and possibly some crack.

I love these things.

"You're my favorite brother," I tell him when he sets the homemade salsa in front of me.

Mark grunts as Sean drops a bowl of hand-dipped chocolate strawberries in the space between us. "Yesterday I was her favorite brother for building those flower boxes off the front of her cabin."

Sean grins and forks a few hunks of pineapple off a fruit plate at the center of the table. "James got to be favorite brother last week when he nailed down my mother's signature on the legal paperwork for the property title," he says. "At least Bree spreads the love around."

James ignores them as well as the food. "All right, guys. Let's take care of business."

He's standing with his hands on the back of a chair like he's calling court to order. It's not a stretch, since he was a high-powered attorney in New York before we got this crazy idea to build a resort together.

James turns to Mark, who just piled six chocolate strawberries on his plate. "Did you get that irrigation glitch figured out on the golf course?"

Mark nods around a mouthful of breakfast burrito and swipes at his beard with a napkin. "Yeah. I've got the parts coming in from Portland tomorrow, but I rigged something up to keep it running until then."

"Well done." James turns to Sean and me. "Is everything handled for that authors' convention next month?"

Authors make me think of Virginia Woolf, which makes me think of Austin, which makes me think of that kiss, and before I know it, I'm miles away from this conversation and back in Hottie Cop's arms.

What the hell was I thinking kissing him like that? And how can I make it happen again?

No. Bad idea.

I order myself to pay attention as Sean rattles off a bunch of details about the special menu he's planning for the authors. Something about an icebox plum cake as a nod to a William Carlos Williams poem, and a butterbeer cocktail for a session on plotting like JK Rowling. I'm only half listening. It's been seventy-two hours since I kissed Officer Hot Hands. Should it bother me that he hasn't called?

You told him you weren't interested, dummy. Why would he call?

"Wasn't Bree planning some special nature hike where they go out in the woods and write about trees?" Mark's voice—and my name—jar me back to the conversation with my brothers.

"Right." I clear my throat. "They're also paying extra for guided yoga on the back lawn every morning, and I think I can get them to sign on for a group spa date midweek."

"Good." James shuffles some papers as Mark helps himself to another handful of strawberries. Considering the size of his hands, the plate is nearly empty, but no one says anything. For once, Mark's perpetual scowl is gone, and he looks like a kid on Halloween morning. A six-foot-five kid with a beard, but still. My brother might resemble an angry lumberjack, but he's got one helluva sweet tooth.

Does Austin like sweets?

Did he grow up with a mom who baked cookies and a dad who coached Little League, or were there more struggles behind the scenes of a law enforcement family? I have to admit, I liked learning about him the other day. About his family and what makes him tick. Did he notice I don't love sharing my own childhood stories? Of course he did. He's a cop, and cops notice everything.

Which is the problem, really. The reason I need to keep my distance.

So why the hell did you kiss him, idiot?

I know, *I know.* It was dumb, okay? One second I'm standing there talking with him about the finer points of sunset dining, and the next second I'm polishing his tonsils with my tongue. I don't know what happened.

I've always been a sucker for big hands. The sight of Austin stroking his huge palm over that—

"Hello! Earth to Bree."

I snap my attention back to the meeting and see my three brothers staring at me.

"Where the hell did you go?" James demands.

"Nowhere." I survey the table to see them all regarding me with skeptical expressions. All of them but Sean, who has an odd little knowing grin. I ignore him and look at Mark. "What?"

"You looked sort of ill for a second," he mutters. "Like you were going to puke."

"I feel fine." I grab my burrito and dunk it in the big bowl of salsa, giving the exercise way more attention than it deserves. I sneak a glance at Sean and see he's still grinning. The jerk knows damn well what a crush looks like, and I hope he's not reading that on my face.

Across the table, James frowns. "Mark said there was a cop out here a couple days ago. Is everything okay?"

Fuck. Leave it to the lawyer to ferret out the one thing I absolutely *don't* want to discuss.

"Everything's fine." More salsa on the burrito, way more. I

should probably grab some of those strawberries, too, before Mark eats them all.

James is frowning harder. "There's not a problem with the city permits? Because if the police have questions about—"

"The permits are fine," I snap. "The cop is fine. Everything's *fine.*"

Sean snort-laughs and I whirl on him. "What?" I demand.

"You." He reaches across Mark and grabs the last strawberry, popping it in his mouth with a Cheshire cat grin. "You've got it bad."

James and Mark frown at me, probably wondering if "it" is contagious. I play dumb. "I don't know what you're talking about, but if we could get back on track with this meeting—"

"I know that look," Sean says. "You're smitten."

"*Smitten?*" Mark snorts. "Who the hell uses words like *smitten?*"

"A guy who knows damn well what it looks like." Sean keeps grinning at me, but James just looks baffled.

"What the hell are you people talking about?" He raps his stack of papers on the table and takes a seat, glaring at the empty strawberry plate. He helps himself to a bunch of grapes instead.

"Amber told me he asked you out," Sean says, still gloating. "She says you shot him down like a dog in the street, but that you seemed to actually like him."

"I'm going to kill Amber," I mutter. "Maybe you, too."

"Who?" James demands. "Who asked you out?"

It's Mark's turn to frown. "Wait. Did you tell him no, and he's not respecting that? Because I could have a word with him about—"

"What the hell are we talking about here?" James demands.

Sean looks positively thrilled at all the shit he's stirred up. "Bree and Austin sittin' in a tree," he sings. "K-i-s-s-i-n—"

"For the love of Christ," I growl and leap across the table to smack his head with my rolled-up napkin. "What are you, six years old? Are you going to start pulling my pigtails and telling me cops have cooties?"

"You're dating a cop?" James stares at me, struggling to put together puzzle pieces that have nothing to do with resort business. This is way outside his comfort zone. "Is that what this is about?"

"No, I'm not dating a cop." I glare at Sean, channeling all my exasperation at him. "Look what you started."

"This is fun," he says. "See what you missed out on not having brothers around when you were growing up?"

Mark nods and shoves half a burrito in his mouth. "We're protecting you."

"If by 'protecting' you mean 'annoying the fuck out of,' you're nailing it," I mutter. "Good job."

James studies me as he dips his spoon into the salsa bowl and carefully ladles some onto his burrito. "I wouldn't have pictured you with a cop."

I shouldn't react. I should change the subject like I always do, but something in his voice has my defenses pricking to attention. "What's that supposed to mean?" I ask. "I'm very virtuous."

I give them my most virtuous look, which doesn't seem convincing. Not to Mark, anyway, who's watching me the way I saw him staring curiously at humping Humane Society dogs at our dog park grand opening when a frisky chihuahua tried to mount a Doberman by climbing on an overturned bucket.

Sean might be the one to recognize the signs of unwelcome lovesickness, but it's Mark who knows me best. Mark who's more likely to pick up on a darker undercurrent. We're only six months apart, since dad's affair with Mark's mother began when I was still a bun in my own mom's oven. It's hard to believe under those circumstances that we'd be close, but we are.

Well, as close as anyone gets to Mark.

He studies me for a long time, long enough to leave me

squirming in my seat. When I finally meet his eyes, he doesn't look away. "What?" I demand. "Do you have something to say?"

Mark rubs a hand over his beard, considering his words. "Be careful."

Yeah. No shit.

But I give him my perfect PR smile and dab my mouth with a napkin. "But of course, brother dearest."

Easier said than done.

CHAPTER 5

AUSTIN

"*T*hat's it, girl," I murmur. "Lick it all off. There you go, just like that."

Virginia Woof slurps the last of the icing off her special made-for-dogs cupcake, while I stand there on the street corner hoping no one heard me talking dirty to my dog.

"Austin?"

Of course.

As the voice recognition software kicks on in my brain, I go from shame to excitement in three-point-six seconds and turn to see Bree Bracelyn walking up the street toward me. She's wearing slim green pants tucked into black boots that make her legs look killer. Her black sweater falls off one shoulder, and I wonder if that's intentional. Fashion isn't my forte, but I'm pretty sure she's not wearing a bra under there. "Bree. You look great."

She beams at me. "Thanks."

Virginia Woof barks her approval, and Bree's gaze swings to the leash in my hand and the shaggy beast hitched to the other end of it. "This is Virginia?"

"Yep," I stoop down to scratch behind her ears, earning myself a fond grunt from my dog. "We're on our way to the dog park by the river."

"If she ever gets tired of the river, you should bring her to the dog park at the resort," she says. "We put in these cool spray fountains that look like fire hydrants. Dogs go nuts for them."

"We'll have to check that out sometime." I straighten up and switch the leash to my other hand.

Virginia yips and wiggles her way up to Bree with her tail smacking the sidewalk. Bree stoops down and laughs. "You've got a little frosting on your face, girl." She pulls a tissue out of her pocket and swipes at my dog's mouth, earning herself a lick on the back of her hand.

I shove my hands in my pockets and try not to feel awkward about Bree kneeling on the ground in front of me. "I worked late three times this week, so I promised her a pupcake for being patient."

Bree sits back on her heels and goes to work scratching Virginia's scruff, zeroing in on my dog's favorite spot right behind her left ear. "You like that, huh?" Bree coos. "You like a good ear scritch, hmmm? Is that the spot, baby? Right there?"

Virginia groans in ecstasy and flops on her back to grant access to her belly. Bree obliges, rubbing circles on the dog's fur-dotted egg belly.

"Pupcakes?" Bree asks, looking up at me with a smile in those bright green eyes.

I jerk a thumb toward Dew Drop Cupcake shop behind me. "They sell cupcakes made just for dogs. I don't know what's in them, but Virginia's crazy about them."

"You came to a cupcake shop just to buy a cupcake for your dog." She grins and shakes her head. "That's either really sweet or a little embarrassing."

"It might be both," I admit. "But I was ordering human cupcakes, too."

"Please tell me those are cupcakes for humans and not some

45

weird cannibalistic treat."

I laugh and order myself to quit looking down the front of her sweater. She's definitely not wearing a bra, but it's none of my business. "I sure hope so, or my niece's birthday party is going to be awkward."

"You have a niece?"

"I have five nieces," I tell her. "My sisters have a talent for producing girl children. Which is perfect, since my parents have a talent for spoiling granddaughters."

Bree gets to her feet, earning a sigh of disappointment from Virginia, but one of relief from me. There's only so much a guy can take when a beautiful woman is kneeling braless at his feet.

She dusts the knees of her pants. "How old is the birthday girl?"

"She turns three on Saturday. It's a princess theme."

"Oooh, I have a bunch of tiaras if you want to borrow them."

"Really?"

"My mother used to make me do these cotillion balls," she says, frowning a little. "I think she hoped I'd magically morph into a cultured lady instead of a socially-awkward dork, but it didn't work out."

"No?" I pretend to size her up, which is really just an excuse to look at her again. God, she's beautiful. "You seem pretty cultured and ladylike to me."

"I was a late-bloomer," she says, cheeks pinkening ever so slightly. "I don't know why I still have the tiaras."

Her face plays out a series of emotions I can't quite read. Nostalgia? Regret? Sadness? She's good at hiding it, but not as good as I am at noticing before her mask slips back into place. "Anyway, your niece can have the tiaras. I might even have some old gowns if she likes playing dress-up."

"You should come to the party." I blurt the words before I think them through, but they feel right, so I keep going. "Wear your tiara and become Ainslie's new best friend."

She laughs and tosses her dark curls. "Thanks, but I don't want to intrude on family stuff."

That wasn't quite a no, and there's a longing in her eyes that tells me she kinda likes the idea. But something tells me I shouldn't push too hard. "I promise everyone would be thrilled," I assure her. "Ainslie loves meeting new grownups."

"I'll think about it." She glances behind her at the cupcake shop. "I should probably continue my mission."

"Any mission that involves cupcakes is a worthwhile mission."

She smiles and I swear that's becoming my favorite sight in the world. "I've got a last-minute request from a bride who wants twelve dozen cactus cupcakes for a high desert-themed wedding rehearsal dinner," Bree says. "I'm seeing what Chelsea can do."

"If she can make pupcakes and princess cupcakes for Ainslie's party, I'm guessing she could manage cactuses." I frown. "Cacti? That's the plural, right?"

"Cacticakes," Bree says, shoving a mess of curls off her forehead. "Do you happen to know if she's single?"

"Who, Chelsea?"

I must look surprised because Bree laughs. "Not for me—I'm straight."

"I kinda figured."

Bree's cheeks pinken again, and she shoves her hands in her pockets. "Yeah, about that—"

"It was the best kiss of your life and you're totally rethinking your position on dating officers of the law?"

Her blush deepens, but she's smiling. "You read my mind."

I wish she weren't kidding.

"Say no more," I play along. "I'll pick you up Friday night for our first date. Do you like Italian? Or do you want to just skip the date and get right to planning our wedding?"

She shakes her head, but she's still laughing. "I should apologize for throwing myself at you like that," she says. "I don't know what came over me."

"You should definitely *not* apologize," I tell her, shifting Virginia's leash from one hand to the other so she can sniff a nearby tree. "It was the highlight of my week."

"That's the problem." She sighs and folds her arms over her chest like she's cold. I consider offering her my jacket, but I'm not wearing one. "I told you I'm not interested, and then I do something dumb like that."

I should probably be hurt that she's calling our kiss dumb. But I've kissed enough women in my life to know that kiss was anything but dumb. It was toe-curling. Amazing. A kiss I'm still feeling almost a week later, and from the look in her eyes, I'm not alone in that.

"It's fine, Bree," I tell her. "We all do crazy things sometimes."

"Not me."

She's so insistent that I give her my skeptical cop eyebrow lift. "Never?"

"Nope," she says. "Totally straight arrow here."

"I find that hard to believe," I say. "You seem like a woman with all kinds of skeletons in your closet. A secret life selling contraband silly string in Alabama—it's illegal there, by the way. Or texting and walking in Hawaii—also illegal."

There's a tiny clench in her jaw, but her smile doesn't waver. I probably would have missed it if I weren't so focused on her mouth and wondering about that raspberry lip stuff. She's wearing it again, and I'm aching to taste it. Taste *her*.

"Of course you're an expert on random-ass laws," she says. "Silly string is seriously illegal in Alabama?"

"Don't look too impressed that I know that," I tell her. "It's just something I was Googling for a presentation I'm giving at the state police convention in a few weeks."

Virginia gives a sharp bark, signaling me that it's time to go. *Damn.*

"It was good seeing you," she says, all business now. All except

48

the part where she totally just checked out my hands. "Take care, Austin."

"You, too," I tell her. "Shout if you change your mind about coming to Ainslie's party. It could be great PR for the resort."

She gives me a dubious look. "How would a three-year-old's birthday party be good for the resort?"

"Because my aunt Genevieve will be there."

I give her a second to connect the dots. It's a perfect opportunity to study her face, to soak in the deep, deep green of her eyes.

Eyes that fly wide open when she finally gets it. "No way!" She slugs me in the shoulder so hard Virginia barks. "Sorry," Bree says, and I'm not sure if she's talking to me or my dog. "You're kidding me. Your aunt is *the* Genevieve Dugan?"

"The one and only," I admit. "Celebrity wedding planner to the stars. You've seen her show?"

"Are you freakin' kidding me? I made Sean binge-watch it with me a few weeks ago when he confessed he's thinking of proposing to Amber. Genevieve is seriously your aunt?"

"On my father's side. You didn't hear this from me, but she's been scouting for some West Coast locations to feature next season."

I am shamelessly using my famous aunt and my three-year-old niece to get a date with this woman, and I'm not even sorry. I probably should be, but—

"I can't believe you're serious." Bree bounces like a kid on Christmas morning, and I know for sure there's no bra under that sweater.

Goddammit.

"I'm totally serious," I say as most of the blood leaves my brain and heads south. "You'd be doing me a big favor by coming as my date. It would save me from being one of the only guys there. Besides, I'm not kidding—she really is looking for more West Coast spots for her show. She told me about it last week, asked if I'd show her around when she's here."

"This could be huge!" She bounces some more. "Oh my God, we could get Amber and Jade in on the action, and maybe they could be featured. *Country chic wedding venues of the high desert* or something like that."

I love how she thinks. That she doesn't regard the venue next door as competitors, but as friends whose business she wants to promote. A rising tide lifts all boats and all that. Just seeing the delight in her eyes makes my heart swell.

My heart isn't the only thing swelling. "Please stop bouncing," I plead, placing a hand on her shoulder. "So, is that a yes on the party?"

"What?" She looks down at the front of her sweater, then smirks. "It's a strapless bra, Officer Pervy."

Busted.

I clear my throat. "I was just looking out for your well-being."

"Sure you were." She grins as her sweater slips farther off her shoulder. She doesn't try to fix it. "What time is the party?"

"Five o'clock on Saturday," I tell her. "How about I pick you up at four-thirty?"

"It's a date."

A date. I try not to feel smug. "But not a *date*-date," I point out. "Because you don't date cops."

Her lashes flutter as her sweater slips again, and all the blood leaves my brain. "Maybe I'll make an exception for cops who buy cupcakes for dogs."

"Who also have famous aunts and super-cute three-year-old nieces?"

"Sure, and nice blue eyes."

I play it cool, not wanting to read too much into the compliment. "You're thinking there might be more than one pupcake-purchasing cop with cute nieces, famous aunts, and blue eyes?"

Bree smiles, and I swear my heart trips over itself. "Let's start with the one."

* * *

ON FRIDAY MORNING at the Dandelion Café, I watch my father speak low into his lapel mike. "I have a visual on the subject. Over."

The response is muffled by his earpiece, but my father nods and replies. "Copy that. Subject is halfway through a Belgian waffle with extra strawberries. Over."

Since I'm sitting on the opposite side of the booth, I can't see who he's looking at. I resist the urge to steal a look behind me and focus on signaling the waitress for a coffee refill.

"Kids never pulled stuff like this back in my day," my dad mutters, but he's got a good-natured smile in place.

I pick up a slice of bacon and bite it in half. "Can't say I remember it, either."

"Nah, you did it once," he says. "Remember? Junior year, you and that wild girl. What was her name?"

"Angelique." I can't believe I forgot. "I think she's married to a teacher now."

My dad nods and takes a sip of his coffee. "You always did like those little Bettie Boop brunettes," he says. "It's no wonder you've got a thing for that resort girl."

I paste on my most neutral cop stare, which does diddly squat for the guy who taught it to me. "We're just friends."

He snorts so hard that his coffee sloshes over the rim when he sets it down. "Sure you are. That's why you're bringing her to Ainslie's party tomorrow?"

"If I were looking to get lucky, you think I'd pick a three-year-old's princess party as my seduction spot?"

My father grins and grabs the other half of my bacon. "I think that's exactly what you'd do. Great idea, too. Let her see you're a good family man."

All right, time for a subject change. I saw off a hunk of my eggs benedict and spear it with my fork. "You saw Ryan Zonski's legal team is moving forward with the appeal?"

My dad's smile disintegrates faster than a snowball doused in hot maple syrup. "Yeah. Sorry about that. I know that case was a tough one for you."

"It's not about me," I say, though my dad already knows this. He's been in the business longer than me and has lived through plenty of gut-wrenching cases. Cases like Ryan Zonski, a strung-out teenager who drove off a cliff with his twin siblings in the car in a murder-suicide plot that went horribly wrong.

More wrong than a regular murder-suicide, that is.

"It's more about the family," I continue. "I don't want them to have to go through that again."

"Any luck finding new witnesses?"

"Yeah." I nod my thanks to the waitress refilling my mug then take a fortifying sip. "Someone in Boston, of all places. A classmate who claims Zonski told her all about his plans before he did it."

"Hmm." My dad looks thoughtful. "Premeditation. How come she never came forward before?"

"Moved out of state with her family in the middle of their sophomore year," I say. "Ended up in rehab a few months later, so she had no idea he actually went through with it."

"Good job tracking her down."

"Thank you."

This. This is why I love having a dad in law enforcement. Someone to bounce ideas around, someone who congratulates me for feats I never explicitly took credit for. He's right, tracking down the new witness was my work, but I don't go around wrenching my arm to pat myself on the back for it. I love that my dad just *knows.*

"Austin, I heard the wonderful news."

I turn to see Mrs. Percy bustling to the table, her salt-and-pepper perm glinting under florescent lights. She co-chairs the

Deschutes Children's Welfare Society with Mrs. Sampson, and the conspiratorial glint in her eye tells me I'm not going to like this conversation any more than I like talking about my love life or suicidal teenagers.

"What good news, Mrs. Percy?"

"That you've agreed to do the calendar." She pats my bicep, taking a page out of Mrs. Sampson's book. "The naughty cops calendar for the children."

Good Lord. "Naughty cops for the children," I repeat. "Please tell me that's not the name of it?"

She gives me a dismissive wrist flick and smiles. "We'll worry about that later. The important thing is that you're doing it." She leans down and lowers her voice. "We might even be able to get you on the cover."

This is far from my greatest career ambition, partly because I never agreed to do the damn calendar. "I think there's been a misunderstanding," I tell her. "I'm not posing for any calendar."

Mrs. Percy's face falls, and she looks at my father. "I thought you said—"

"We'll talk about it." My father gives her his campaign grin and winks. "Great scones, by the way. Lacey made them for breakfast yesterday and said you gave her the recipe."

"Yes, well." She preens a little. "We'll be in touch."

Mrs. Percy walks away, but not before ogling my chest and murmuring something about my abs. Christ.

"Thanks a lot," I mutter to my dad. "Are you my pimp now?"

My dad grins and forks up a piece of pancake. "You're a creative thinker," he says. "That's why you're in line to be chief. You'll figure out some way to make everyone happy."

"Somehow, I doubt that involves me taking off my clothes." The second the words leave my mouth, my brain zips straight to Bree. I can't wait to see her later. Even if it's just a kid's birthday party, even if she's got this no-cop rule, even if—

"Subject is on the move." My father barks the word into his

lapel mike and stands up. He takes one last swig of coffee and heads for the door, leaving me to get the bill. I shove two twenties under my plate and the last piece of bacon in my mouth before following my dad out onto the sidewalk.

He's already mid-conversation with a nervous-looking blonde girl who can't be more than sixteen. My father is frowning with his thumbs looped over his belt. The girl looks at him, then at me. We're both in uniform.

"We have a reason to believe you're dealing weapons to terrorists, young lady," my father says. "Possibly smuggling aircraft carriers, too."

"What?" The girl gives a nervous laugh, then stops. "No, I— this has to be some mistake."

"Unlikely." My father folds his arms over his chest as the girl's gaze shifts to me. I almost feel bad playing along, but I fix my expression into a cop scowl and let my dad take the lead.

The girl swallows and reaches for her phone. "I just need to call—"

"Ma'am, please keep your hands where we can see them."

The girl's smile wobbles. My father must see that, too, because he unfolds his arms and softens his voice as he gestures to her car. "I'm sure we can clear this up easily. Ma'am, I'm going to need you to open your trunk."

"My—my trunk?"

"What's that?" My father touches his earpiece like he's getting a call, even though I can tell he's faking it. He glances at the girl. "Subject is a Caucasian female, sixteen years old—"

"Seventeen," the girl says, fiddling nervously with her keys.

God, I hope we get this over with soon.

"Subject appears to be unarmed," my father continues, "but with advanced martial arts training and a history of violence—"

"What?" The girl looks frantic now. "I don't know any martial arts."

"If you like, we can clear this up down at the jailhouse," my father says.

"Jail? But I—"

"Please, ma'am—let's do this the easy way and have a look in the trunk."

The girl swallows and walks around to the back of her car. As she jams a key into the hole, a mop-haired boy in a rumpled gray suit approaches from the other side of the street. He has a dozen red roses in one hand and a nervous look on his face.

I don't blame him. A stunt like this could go sideways in a hurry.

There's an audible gasp from the girl as the trunk pops open, and a dozen helium balloons fly out. The girl sticks a tentative hand inside and pulls out a cardboard sign. I peer over her shoulder at the red words scrawled across it.

"You've arrested my heart," she reads aloud. *"Will you go to homecoming with me?"*

She looks up at the boy, and her face transforms from terror to delight in the space of ten seconds. For a second, I think he's going to drop to one knee, but no, that's not how this goes.

It's homecoming season—second only to promposal season in craziness—and this teenage Romeo just pulled off one helluva surprise invitation. Can't say I'm in favor of the fear factor, but the kid gets props for execution.

"The boy's dad is on the force," my father mutters to me as the girl throws her arms around the kid's ruddy neck. "Asked me to do this as a favor."

The girl is sobbing in earnest now, but it's happy tears. If I was pissed at my dad a few seconds ago for scaring the shit out of this poor girl, I can admit now it may have been worth it.

"Yes, I'll go to homecoming with you," the girl bawls. "Oh my God, I'm going to kill you."

"Ma'am," my father says. "Threatening homicide in front of two officers of the law is inadvisable."

My father grins, and I catch myself smiling back.

CHAPTER 6

BREE

I don't know why I expect Austin to show up in a police car to pick me up for a kid's birthday party. It's not like it's never dawned on me he has a life outside being a cop.

But I'm still surprised to see him pull up in a vintage Volvo. I don't know much about cars, but this one looks a few years older than I am. That's judging from the body style, anyway. As soon as he opens the passenger door for me, I can see the leather seats are immaculate, and the dashboard is a high-polished shrine to '80s automotive technology.

"Cool car," I say, ducking down for a better look. "Very retro."

"Thanks," he says. "I have a truck for camping and stuff, but the Volvo thing is kind of a hobby."

"What do you mean?"

"Restoring vintage Volvos," he says. "This girl is my fifth."

I find it ridiculously endearing that his car is female and that he's clearly fond of her. "Does she have a name?"

"Tallulah," he says without hesitation. "It's Swedish."

I laugh as he hands me in through the passenger side and closes the door behind me. Such a gentleman. He strides around the front of the car and gets behind the wheel, but he doesn't start the car right away.

"I dated a guy my freshman year in college who drove a Volvo." I don't mention it was a souped up brand new one with all the bells and whistles, or that his parents bought it for him. "He called it the Swedish Love Machine."

Austin gives me a pained look. "And you think dating a cop would be a step down from that?"

"Good point." I bite my lip. "For the record, it's not about stepping down or up or—well, anything like that."

"What is it about?"

I glance down at my lap, twirling my fingers in the ribbons of the package I've wrapped for Ainslie. "Maybe I'm afraid of dating someone who gets shot at?"

Hey, it's a good reason. It's the one I always hear in books and movies when women are reluctant to date soldiers or cops or anyone else with a dangerous job.

But when I look up, I see Officer Hot Stuff isn't buying it. "I'm in a supervisory role," he says. "The last time someone shot at me, it was one of my deputies with a marshmallow gun. This is rural Central Oregon, not Southside Chicago."

And this isn't the real issue anyway. I know it. He knows it. We're both just beating around the bush. "I shouldn't have kissed you," I murmur. "I'm sorry if I'm sending mixed signals."

Austin lifts a hand and brushes a curl off the side of my face. Every nerve in my cheek sizzles to life like a sparkler. "So you regret it?"

I bite my lip, not ready to go that far. Truth be told, that kiss was the highlight of my month. "I feel guilty for yanking you around."

"Honey, you can yank me around anytime you want."

I laugh and twirl the sparkly pink gift ribbons around my thumb. "I wasn't being fair to you."

Lame. Lame that I'm sitting here telling him how I shouldn't have kissed him while every nerve in my body is screaming for him to kiss me again.

Those blue-grey eyes hold mine, and I swear he just read my mind. "How about I even things out?"

"H—how?" My response comes out breathy, and I hate how much I want him to touch me again.

"If I kiss you, you can stop kicking yourself over kissing me."

I nod, even though that makes about as much sense as shooting yourself in the right foot because you've already shot the left one. Still, I hear myself breathing, "Okay."

"Okay?" He sounds surprised.

"Okay," I repeat. "That's reasonable."

It's not even remotely reasonable, but it's not rational thought driving either of us right now. Austin cups the side of my face in his hand and draws me closer. I go willingly, practically falling into him. I close my eyes and breathe him in, wanting to savor it this time. The last kiss happened so fast.

He's gentle at first, barely brushing my lips with his. I reach for the back of his head, aching to feel more of him. Aching for a lot more than a kiss.

He responds by grazing my tongue with his, still deliciously gentle. I groan and deepen the kiss, not content to make this a perfunctory smooch. I open my eyes, startled to see he's looking at me, too. His blue-gray eyes lock with mine, and he smiles against my mouth. Breaking the kiss, he rests his forehead against mine, still holding the back of my head.

"What are you thinking, Bree Bracelyn?" he asks.

I'm thinking I want to climb over the gear shift and straddle you like a porn star right now.

"We—we should probably go," I murmur.

"Probably." He doesn't let go of me. I don't want him to.

Slowly, I touch my lips to his again. His eyes flutter closed, and he kisses me again, rougher this time. He grips the curve of my waist, and I arch into him, begging him with my body to touch me. To lift his hand a few more inches. To graze the underside of my breast with one of those massive hands.

He breaks the kiss again, and this time his eyes are wild and full of heat. "We should definitely go." His voice is gravelly. "I don't want to have to explain to my three-year-old niece that I'm late to her party because I was ripping your clothes off in the front seat of my car."

"Oh. Yes—that would be—bad."

"Not really." Austin draws back and starts the car then shoots me a grin. "But now's not the right time."

When is the right time? I want to ask, but I don't think my mouth works anymore. Is this what they mean by kissed senseless? I'm pretty sure that's what Austin just did, and I want him to do it again.

But goddamn it, I said I wouldn't. I have tons of good reasons for that, and I'll remember them just as soon as my head stops spinning.

Austin eases the car down the resort driveway, and I go back to twirling my fingers in the ribbons. Austin's the first to break the silence.

"You got Ainslie a gift?"

"I hope she likes superheroes," I say. "It's a dress-up kit that has a few different kinds of capes and masks and accessories and stuff. I poked around online and I guess this is all the rage with the kiddie crowd right now. They had a bunch of them at the toy store downtown."

"She'll love it," he says. "You didn't have to do that, but she'll be thrilled."

"I remember what it's like to have a birthday party where no one showed up with presents."

Or no one showed up at all. I don't say that part out loud, but I wonder if Austin reads anything into my silence. I hurry to fill it. "So is there anything I should know about your family?"

He grins and eases the car out onto the highway that leads

toward town. "They're loud, nosy, and really annoying. Also, I love them to death."

I laugh and slip my sunglasses out of my purse. It's less about the sun's glare and more that I don't want him to see how mind-whacked I still am from that kiss. "So pretty much a typical family."

"Yep," he says. "Get ready to be asked lots of awkward questions. I already told them we're friends, but none of them believe me."

I slip a hand back into my purse and pull out a tissue. He keeps his eyes on the road as I reach over and wipe a smear of my lipstick off the corner of his mouth. "There," I tell him. "At least now you're a little more believable."

He grins and steers down a narrow side road. "Don't count on it. My dad's a better cop than I am. If anyone's hiding anything, he always figures it out."

I swallow hard, grateful he can't see my eyes. "Good to know."

AUSTIN'S FAMILY is everything he said they'd be and more. Ainslie is freakin' adorable and keeps planting herself on my lap and adjusting the tiara she insisted I wear the second I walked through the door.

"Do you like camels?" she asks with an earnestness that has me grinning.

"I do like camels," I say. "Very much. How about you?"

"I, too, like camels."

I could seriously gobble her up. "How about reindeer? I have some friends with a big herd of reindeer."

"Santa?" Her eyes go wide, and it occurs to me I should have thought this through. Amber and Jade hired my cousin, Brandon, to be Santa last year at their ranch. The sisters spend the Christmas season playing up the whole Santa-and-his-reindeer thing, but I'm not totally sure how they explain things in the off-season.

"The reindeer stay here on a ranch when Santa's back at the North Pole," I say, hoping that's vague enough. "They—uh—do special flight training when it's not Christmastime."

I lift my gaze to find Austin's sister, Kim, offering a reassuring smile. "We went out there last December to get our picture taken with Santa and the reindeer," she says. "Ainslie learned all about them."

"Mom, remember how Vixen *pooped*?" Clearly this was the highlight of Ainslie's young life, and she bounces off my lap to go tell Austin about it.

I follow her with my eyes, watching as he interrupts his conversation with his father and brother-in-law to kneel down and talk with Ainslie. I'm not even sure I ever want children but seeing the way he holds eye contact with her, the way he listens to her story like it's the most fascinating thing he's ever heard—I'm seriously feeling my ovaries twist.

Kim leans closer to me on the couch. "He's always so great with kids," she says. "Someone needs to hurry up and make my brother a daddy."

I turn to face her and get the sense she might be interviewing me for the job. "He'd be a good father," I manage, giving her my best PR smile.

Not that I know what a good father looks like. My dad may have gifted me a ranch, but I can count on one hand the number of times he gave me a hug or remembered my birthday or—*no.* I'm not going down this poor-little-rich-girl path.

Time to redirect the conversation. "How did you and Ainslie's dad meet?"

Kim smiles and looks over at the tight knot of men conversing across the room. Since the knot includes Austin, it's a great excuse to watch him again.

"Brian and I were college sweethearts," Kim says. "We've actually been married almost twelve years, but it took a lot of trying before Ainslie came along."

"She's adorable."

I feel for couples with fertility challenges, but there's something about the notion of "trying" that always makes me picture the couple with matching sweatbands and a coach's whistle having exuberantly competitive, sweaty sex.

This is not the picture I need in my head right now, so I keep my eyes on Austin, figuring he's a good distraction.

"God, I hope Meredith doesn't marry Eddie," Kim whispers. "Baby sister doesn't have the best track record."

"Eddie's the guy talking to Austin right now?"

Kim nods. "Meredith has a habit of picking absolutely horrible guys."

"Horrible like—dangerous?"

Kim shakes her head, then shrugs. "Not dangerous, though Austin or my dad will usually do a background check on Meredith's dates. They did the same thing for our other sister, Katie, before she got married. I need to remember to ask Austin if he's done one yet for Eddie."

I swallow hard, hoping Kim doesn't notice the waver in my smile. "He does background checks on people you date?"

"Yeah." Kim laughs. "Our dad did it, too, back when I was in college. He ran one for every guy I dated before Brian."

"Does that freak you out or make you feel safer?"

"Oh, definitely safer." She smiles. "Being in a family of cops, you know they've got your back no matter what."

It must be good to have that level of security. To know someone loves and supports you no matter what. My siblings and I weren't close growing up, but I like to think we're building that now.

"How did you and Austin meet?" Kim asks.

I lift the glass of pink lemonade Ainslie brought me earlier and take a small sip. "Austin came to our VIP event at Ponderosa Resort a couple weeks ago."

"Oh, so it's a new relationship?" Her eyebrows do a hopeful lift.

"I wouldn't call it a *relationship*, exactly."

"Honey, you're looking at him like he's an ice cream cone on a hot day." She laughs when I open my mouth to protest. "Don't worry, he's doing the same to you," Kim adds. "I'm just saying, those aren't friendly sort of looks."

My cheeks go hot, and I wonder who else has noticed. Is it that obvious I want to jump Hottie Cop's bones?

My answer comes in the form of Genevieve Dugan, celebrity wedding planner extraordinaire, who comes sailing into the room with a tray lined with more glasses of pink lemonade. She makes a beeline for Kim and me, jostling us both as she plunks down on the sofa between us.

"I found the vodka," she announces, handing us each a glass. "One for you, Kimmycakes, and one for Bree-who-says-she's-not-Austin's-girlfriend-but-totally-wants-to-tear-off-his-clothes."

So much for subtlety. I grimace and accept the lemonade then take a dainty sip.

"Thank you." For the lemonade, not the awkward intrusion into my innermost thoughts. But hell, Austin did warn me. "Do you make it out to Central Oregon very often, Genevieve?"

"I've only visited a few times. It's certainly changed over the years." She takes a drink of her own lemonade and gives me her trademark smile I've seen dozens of times on TV. "I remember visiting in the late nineties when the city was a half-dead former mill town with about thirty thousand people."

"What are we up to now, about ninety thousand?" Kim asks.

I nod, grateful my resort-opening research has given me something to contribute to the conversation. "It was about ninety-two thousand in town with the last census, but we see about twenty-five thousand tourists a day during peak summer season."

Genevieve smiles and swirls the ice cubes in her lemonade. "And I'm guessing that was a factor in your decision to open a resort?"

"You must have been talking to Austin." I shoot him a grateful look, relieved he provided the foreplay to my conversation with his uber-famous aunt. He flashes me a smile that shoots straight to my toes and makes me miss the first part of what Genevieve says next.

"...with the destination wedding market?" She looks at me expectantly, and I consider fudging a response to hide the fact that I totally tuned out.

But I might as well come clean. "I'm sorry, I was ogling your nephew and totally missed the first half of that. Would you mind repeating the question?"

The two women bust out laughing, and Genevieve nudges Kim, nearly sloshing her lemonade over the rim of the glass. "I knew I liked her."

The conversation continues from there, with Genevieve asking questions about our capacity, the facilities, and the big-picture vision for Ponderosa Luxury Ranch Resort. I chatter happily about my favorite thing in the world, while doing my best to ignore the guy who's quickly becoming my second favorite thing. How did that happen?

"It looks amazing." Genevieve taps the screen of my iPhone, which I've pulled up to show her some of the resort's stock photos. "I'd definitely love to take a look. Can we set something up in the next few days?"

"Absolutely. I'll clear my whole schedule for you, and I can make sure Jade and Amber are open at the reindeer ranch, too."

"Perfect. I'll be in touch." Genevieve pockets the business card I've handed her as Austin ambles over carrying the half-full bottle of IPA he's been nursing all afternoon.

"Ladies." He nods to the tray of empty glasses on Genevieve's lap. "Vodka?"

"Can't get away with anything in a family full of cops." Genevieve giggles and sets the tray on the coffee table before standing to wrap her arms around her nephew. "Don't worry, it's just a little splash. Your girl is still perfectly sober and capable of consent."

"Jesus, Aunt Genevieve." Kim shakes her head, but the look she shoots her aunt is more fondness than dismay. "Austin, were you there the night of my senior prom when dad pulled my date aside and gave him a talk about drinking and sex and respect for women and God knows what else?"

Austin looks pained. "Was this while Genevieve was giving you the talk about demanding at least one orgasm before he gets his?" He shudders. "I'm still traumatized."

Kim laughs. "That's right, you *were* there. And when you tried to escape, she told you that learning to pleasure a woman is the single greatest skill you could develop."

"I was twelve," he says, shaking his head. "At that point, I was more interested in honing my skills at Mario Kart."

Genevieve gives me a wink before stooping down to gather the tray of empty glasses. "Don't worry, Bree. Odds are good my nephew eventually took my advice to heart."

The look Austin gives me is pure heat and leaves little doubt that Aunt Genevieve is spot on. I cross my legs, reminding myself of all the reasons I should keep my distance. That I'm protecting a lot more than my heart.

But the organ in question isn't the only one that bursts into a flaming ball of need as he smiles at me. It's a smile that's full of promise, and my heart trips over itself to sign on the dotted line for whatever the hell he's offering.

Lord, I'm in trouble.

CHAPTER 7

AUSTIN

The sky is a big swath of star-speckled velvet as I drive Bree home from the birthday party. She's more relaxed than she was on the drive out, and I'm pretty sure it's not just the vodka.

"I only had one of those spiked lemonades," she assures me, even though I haven't asked. "I'm not much of a drinker. Even with wine—which I love—I seldom have more than a glass."

"No judgement here," I assure her, not sure why she's worried about it. "I would have knocked back another beer or two if I weren't driving."

She shifts in her seat, making her chocolate-colored skirt hitch higher up her thigh. It hits below her knees when she's standing, so I love that there's a lot more flesh visible when she's sitting here in the passenger seat of my car. What would it be like to reach over and rest a hand on her knee? To push that skirt up and keep going, to glide my fingers beneath—

"Tell me about your senior prom," she says.

The question catches me off-guard, and it takes me a second to even remember the event. When I do, I can't help feeling a little embarrassed. "I went with a girl I'd known since middle school," I say. "Stacey Fleming. She's a teacher now. Anyway, back then she had, uh... a reputation."

"For putting out?"

Bree's tone is neutral, so I can't tell if she thinks I'm an asshole or what.

"Yeah, I guess." I clear my throat. "I was still a virgin at that point, and I had it in my head that maybe she was my ticket to losing my v-card before graduation."

"And did it work?" She folds her hands in her lap, and the primness in her answer suggests I'm walking the thin line between "horny teenage boy" and "insensitive user of women."

I'm grateful that my honest answer will likely tip me back into the former zone. "Nope," I admit. "Not even close. I was too chickenshit to make a move. Plus, she snuck a flask of tequila in her purse, so I spent the whole evening trying to keep her safe and out of trouble."

"Wow." Bree eyes me in the dimness of the cab. "That's noble of you. So you graduated a virgin, huh?"

I turn the car onto the side road that leads to her place. "I didn't say that."

"Who was the lucky girl?"

I laugh and shake my head. "I'm not naming names. Let's just say she was older, and she taught me some very useful lessons."

Bree grins. "So you took Aunt Genevieve's advice to heart."

"More or less."

"I've wondered what it would have been like," she says. "Going to prom. Having a normal teenage existence."

There's a wistful twist in her voice that makes me glance over. Her hands are still on her lap, balled up in the folds of her skirt. I wonder if a girl like Bree Bracelyn would have given me the time of day in high school.

"If it makes you feel better, I'm betting your education put mine to shame," I tell her. "I don't know much about boarding schools, but I'm guessing there's a reason parents pay good money to get their kids into places like that."

"I suppose so," she says. "Though I'm not sure academic stuff is always the reason."

I start to ask about other reasons but stop myself. She's got that ramrod-straight posture again, and the look that tells me I'm not getting any closer. I decide not to push my luck.

I turn the car onto the asphalt road leading to the resort. The buildings are lit up—the Cedar Golf Club, the Aspen Springs Day Spa—but I cruise past them en route to Bree's cabin.

"Do all of your siblings live here?"

She laughs and does a funny little shrug. "Not everyone, but most of us running the place. That was sort of the deal when we decided to turn Dad's ranch into a resort."

"What do you mean?"

"There was—a substantial inheritance," she says carefully. "Not just the land, but barns and outbuildings and a few cabins that had been built for ranch hands. We remodeled those and then started building more."

"So you could each have your own place?"

"Pretty much. I guess we figured some of us might eventually get married and start families, that sort of thing. We built with that in mind."

I haven't seen the inside of Bree's place, but there's something touching about knowing it was constructed with a future family as part of her plan. Is that what she wants?

"Your cousin lives here, too, right—Brandon?"

"Right. He did tons of construction work for free, so we ended up just giving him his cabin. That'll probably go into the rental pool after he and Jade get married."

I hadn't realized they were actually engaged, or maybe Bree's just assuming. She's closer to the sisters than I am. "Brandon's moving into Jade and Amber's place?"

"It makes the most sense. Jade's more hands-on with the

animals, so she's not going anywhere. I'm guessing Amber will eventually move out and live here with Sean, so she'll still be close to her sister and their business."

"That's handy, falling in love with the neighbor," he says. "My sister, Katie—the one you didn't meet tonight?"

"The one with four girls?"

"Exactly," I say, secretly pleased she's already learned my family. "Her husband's from Minnesota, so they all live there. It's tough on my mom not getting to see them as often."

"You, too, I'm guessing?"

"Yeah. We're a pretty close family."

"I noticed." She smiles, and there's something wistful in that, too. "I always wished for that. Growing up, I mean. I got it a little late in life."

"Your brothers seem pretty cool." *And terrifying*, I add silently, recalling Mark's look of silent disdain. "Sean seems really nice."

"He is," she says. "They're all great. Infuriating sometimes, but I love them."

I pull up in front of her place and kill the lights. The faint yip of coyote song carries through the car windows, so I roll mine down to hear better. There's a full-on orchestra of frogs croaking and a creek burbling somewhere nearby. They're sounds I grew up with, but I'm guessing this is still new to Bree. I turn to see her watching me in the half-light.

"I had a good time today," she says. "Thanks for inviting me."

"I hope it was helpful. With Genevieve, I mean. I hope that turns into something."

She unhooks her seatbelt but doesn't reach for the door. Instead, she turns in her seat to face me and gives me a smile that turns my chest cavity into dough. "I didn't agree to come just so I could meet your aunt."

"Why did you come?" I hold my breath, hoping for a certain answer.

"Because I like spending time with you."

There it is, exactly what I'd hoped to hear. It's all I can do not to pump my fist like a teenage football star.

Bree looks down and fiddles with a thread on the hem of her skirt. "You're a good guy, Austin Dugan."

"Thanks." I think. Did I just get friend-zoned?

Her eyes lift to mine, and the heat there is anything but friend zone. I should kiss her. I should kiss her right now. I should—

"Is that smoke?" Bree's eyes go wide, and she looks around the car, sniffing.

"I smell it, too."

She looks around, frantic. "Is something burning in the car?"

"No, that's not it." I turn to my cracked window and breathe deeply, frowning. "It's outside. It's—"

"My cabin!" Bree shoves open her car door and sprints up her walkway.

I'm a few steps behind her, slowed by my still-latched seatbelt and the fact that she figured it out before I did. We're halfway up the path when I notice the door is ajar.

"Bree, wait," I urge. "Don't go in—your front door—"

"Oh, God." She pounds up the front steps, ignoring my warning. "It's my fault. I totally forgot—"

"Yeah, you did." A hulking, bearded figure clad in lumberjack plaid steps into the doorframe.

Mark. Bree's brother. And he's holding a fire extinguisher.

He puts out a hand to halt her in her tracks. "It's fine. Everything's good. I got it out."

Bree bursts into tears. "It's all my fault," she sobs. "I lit a candle, and I totally forgot about it."

Mark looks utterly dumbfounded, like he's never seen a woman cry before. "Uh, hey." He drags her awkwardly against his chest and pats her back. "It's fine. The only thing that burned is that ugly tablecloth thing. Don't cry. Please don't cry."

The helpless befuddlement on his face is almost comical, and he meets my eye with a look of utter terror. "Here," he says, pushing her away as gently as possible. "Why don't you let the cop take you in. You'll see, everything's okay."

Bree sniffs and steps back, running a hand down the front of his shirt. "I got snot on you."

"It'll wash out."

"Mark, I can't ever thank you enough—"

"Yeah, you can." He frowns. "You can quit crying and go inside where it's warm." He chucks her under the chin then starts down the path with the fire extinguisher in his hand.

"Stay safe, kids," he calls over his shoulder.

Then he vanishes into the darkness. Bree turns to me and sniffs again. "He's not used to seeing me cry."

"Not at your dad's funeral?"

She shakes her head a little sadly. "I cried after, and a lot by myself. But not there."

I put an arm around her, not sure if she needs comfort or reassurance. "Come on. Let's take a look at the damage."

She nods and leads me inside. The smell of fresh cedar mingles with the thick odor of smoke and something oddly fruity.

"Apple blossoms and oak." Bree stares forlornly at a rustic wood table with a charred edge and a pile of foam in the middle of it. She looks up at me with a mascara smudge under one eye. "That was the fragrance of the candle."

"It's uh—nice."

She shakes her head and looks like she might be on the verge of tears again. "I almost never use real candles. I have a zillion of the battery-powered kind, but I wanted something that smelled nice for a change. God, I'm such an idiot."

"You're not an idiot. You have an MBA, and you're one of the driving forces behind a gazillion-dollar resort that shows every sign of being a brilliant idea. You are definitely not an idiot."

I can tell she doesn't believe me. She stares down at the foamy wreckage of her side table and sighs. "I even thought twice about lighting it. I was like, 'is it really a good idea to have an open flame in a house made entirely of wood?' But I was so sure I'd remember to put it out. God, I'm dumb."

"Bree, quit." I grab her hand and pull her away from the mess. "Come on. You're not dumb. We all do dumb things sometimes, but that doesn't make us dumb."

She lets me tow her toward the couch. There's a laptop open on the coffee table, and the screen flickers to life when she bumps it with her hip. I catch the words "juvenile records" at the top of a website before she pushes the laptop shut and drops onto the couch beside me. My cop antennae tingle, but she did mention googling gift ideas for kids.

I have bigger issues at the moment. "It's okay," I tell her. "Your house is safe, you're safe, and there's hardly any damage."

"Name one thing."

"What?"

She looks up at me, green eyes still watery. "Name one thing you've done in your whole life that was this dumb, Officer McPerfect."

"That's easy," I say, ignoring the nickname as I hold out my left hand and tip it sideways to show the edge of my middle finger. "See that scar?"

Bree reaches out and brushes a finger over it. "This?"

I nod. "I can't feel that, by the way. You touching me." Damn shame.

She looks up at me. "What is it?"

"It's a scar from a third-degree burn. I got it when I ignited my own hand *on purpose* when I was sixteen."

"What?" Her expression is equal parts horrified and amused, but at least she no longer looks humiliated.

"Yeah, it's this magic trick my friends used to do."

"This doesn't look very magical." She's still touching my hand, and I'm grateful. Her touch is light, and I can feel it butterfly-soft outside the edges of the scar.

"It wasn't very magical," I admit, dropping my hand to my lap. "You spread rubber cement on your hand and light it on fire. The flame burns the cement, but not your hand. In theory, anyway."

"You might need another theory." Bree traces a finger over my scar again, inching higher up my arm and back down again.

"I used too much rubber cement. My father still hasn't let me live down the fact that he had to come pick up his son who intentionally ignited his own hand."

"Okay, you're right." Bree giggles and drops her hand. "That's pretty dumb."

"Thank you."

"Thank *you*." She smiles, and my damn heart flops over like an excited beagle. "I do feel better."

"Want another?"

"There's more?"

"Sure, I could go all night." Bree's eyes flicker, but I ignore my own accidental innuendo and try to come up with another dose of comfort for her. I settle back on the couch, throwing my arm over the back of it. She settles against me, getting comfortable, too.

"Let's see," I say. "There's the time I went to a concert in Portland a few years ago, and I accidentally walked into the women's restroom."

"Whoops." She shifts on the sofa, bumping my thigh with hers. God, she feels good.

"Yeah. I thought I was so smart ducking out of the show a couple minutes early to beat the rush, and I was the first one into the stall. That should have been my first clue—no urinals."

"What did you do?"

"I was already locked in the stall when I heard the voices and saw the shoes and put two and two together to realize where I was. But by then the line was out the door, and I couldn't escape."

Bree laughs. "So did you stay in there all night?"

"Nope. I finally got the balls to push open the door and walk out, apologizing the whole way. A few ladies yelled at me, but most of them laughed. One even high-fived me."

Bree smiles and snuggles closer. Her shoulder is warm next to mine, and her skirt slides up her bare thigh as she rearranges her legs beneath her. "I don't know if I'd call that dumb," she says. "Definitely embarrassing, though."

"Oh, I can do dumb. Let's see." I give it some thought. "Okay, here's a more recent one—this was just last week at Macy's when I went in to buy my mom a birthday gift."

"What did you get her?"

"Perfume," I say. "Her favorite."

"Such a good son."

"I try." My fingers graze the edge of her bare knee, and she doesn't draw back. "Anyway, I'm walking toward the perfume counter when I bump into this woman. I said, 'oh, I'm sorry, pardon me.'"

"That's not dumb, that's polite."

"It would be if she were a real person. It turned out she was a mannequin."

Bree brings her hands to her mouth to cover her laughter. "That's awesome."

"Oh, it gets worse. I realized I'd just apologized to a mannequin, so I said, 'I'm sorry, I thought you were a real person.' That's when the perfume counter lady walked by."

Bree is practically rolling on the couch laughing. "What did she say?"

"Not a word. She just shot me this really weird look and gave me a wide berth as she walked away."

She's howling with laughter now. It's so much better than the tears earlier, so I try to think of another one.

"Okay, I've got one." Bree thrusts out her hand, spreading her fingers wide across my thigh. "See that scar right there?"

I nod and trace a finger over it. She shivers under my touch. "How did you do it?"

"Paring knife, sixth grade. I was home alone for the first time, and I decided I wanted a baked potato. Only I'd never made one before. I'd only seen my nanny do it, or sometimes the maid."

"You had a nanny and a maid?"

She nods and makes a face. "I know, I know...poor little rich girl."

"I wasn't going to say that at all." I catch her hand before she can pull it back, rubbing my thumb across the scar. "So, what happened?"

"Well, when I'd watched Matilda—that was my nanny—she always stabbed the potato a couple times before she put it in the oven."

"Sure, so it doesn't explode."

"Right. But instead I stabbed my hand."

"Ouch."

"It bled all over the place, but by then, I was sort of in shock. So, I left this trail of blood to the oven and shoved it in and waited for it to get done. Only no one ever told me you had to turn the oven *on*."

"Oh, no."

"By the time my mom got home, I'd bled through a dish towel and gone into shock, and my potato was still ice cold."

I rub the scar, wishing for some way to erase it from her personal history. "Did you go to the hospital?"

"Yeah. It took seven stitches. I always tell people that's why I've never learned to cook."

Her eyes lock with mine and hold. I'm still holding her hand, still stroking the scar with my thumb. Bree's lips part, her chest rising and falling quicker now. My senses fill with the scent of raspberries and oak-moss, and there's a faint buzzing in my ears.

"Austin?"

"Yeah?"

"Whose turn is it to kiss first?"

The words shoot straight to my groin, and it takes me a second to answer. "Want to flip a coin?"

She bites her lip, shaking her head. "Let's meet in the middle."

And so we do, our mouths moving together, lips colliding, tongues tangling, as I let go of her hand and thread my fingers into her hair.

CHAPTER 8

BREE

*H*ow *does this keep happening?*

That's the thought playing on a loop in my brain as my lips collide again with Sergeant Sexypants' delicious mouth, and I find myself falling into another one of his toe-curling kisses.

Not that I'm fighting it. Hell, I might be the one who started it, which just goes to show I'm a wanton floozy who makes terrible life choices.

But this doesn't feel terrible. It feels pretty damn amazing, honestly, and I slide my fingers around the back of his head to make sure he keeps doing it. That he can't pull away or come up for air or do anything except kiss me until we're both dizzy.

One of his great big palms finds its way to my bare knee, and I draw in a sharp breath.

Please move up. Please keep going. Just a few more inches.

The dirty angel whispering words from my left shoulder is an even bigger floozy than I am, but I can't blame her. His touch is amazing, just the right balance of firm and gentle. His hand starts to move, and I swoon like a goddamn teenager.

Keep it together, Bree.

That's the good angel talking, the one I usually listen to like she's my own personal muse. But her voice is muffled now, like the dirty angel stuffed a pair of gym socks in her mouth.

Keep going, Mister Policeman. Keep that hand moving up my skirt and—

Austin must hear the bad angel talking, or maybe he's just as hungry as I am for more of our body parts to become acquainted with each other. His palm slides firm and possessive up my thigh, disappearing beneath the hem of my skirt.

I give a groan of encouragement and press against him, brushing his tongue with mine as our kiss turns more intense. I'm gripping the back of his head like I'm afraid he'll get away, so I let one hand drop to the front of his shirt.

Buttons. We know how these work, don't we?

Honestly, my brain is too fuzzy to recall, and I'm half tempted to tear them open with my teeth. That's how desperate I am to touch him.

Austin groans against my mouth as my fingers find their way into the front of his shirt. I only mean to undo one, but somehow three pop open with a few fast flicks of my thumb and forefinger. Before I know it, I'm stroking my fingers through his chest hair like it's the first time I've ever touched a male chest that wasn't manscaped to bare skin.

Actually, that's true. I've never touched a man with a soft pelt of gloriously perfect chest hair before, and I can't get enough of it. My greedy fingers fondle and stroke and delight in exploring this unexpectedly silky terrain. His pecs are sculpted and hard, just like you'd expect from a cop who's being hounded to strip for a sexy calendar. But the feel of that soft layer of downy hair is like icing on top of a perfect cupcake. My mouth waters, my palms ache with the urge to press and stroke and memorize every muscular curve.

"Bree," he groans against my mouth.

The word startles me, nearly as much as the thought that he's as ravenous for my flesh as I am for his. That's underscored by the fact that his hand just moved another few inches up my thigh to bring his fingertips achingly close to the edge of my undies.

Just a millimeter more. Please.

My whole body's begging for it. I can't take it anymore. I shift on the couch, enough to press the silky center of my panties against his fingertips.

Austin gives a low growl in the back of his throat and nips at my lower lip. "You're making me crazy," he murmurs, but doesn't stop.

His fingers slip beneath the elastic edge of my panties and graze my molten core. I go off like a goddamn rocket.

"God, Austin." I press against him, urging him on. "Don't stop."

He obeys, kissing me harder as the tips of his fingers play me like a violin. Or a piano. Or whatever instrument requires an unbelievable amount of dexterity, that perfect touch of soft and firm. I hadn't realized how slippery-wet turned on I am until Austin's middle finger makes the slow, tortuous journey the entire length of me.

He teases at first, swirling, stroking, coming dangerously close to that tight, sensitive bundle of nerves before backing off again and moving away. I'm practically electrified, waiting for the touch I know is coming. Does he want me to beg?

"Austin, please." I'm not proud. I'm already throwing myself at him, so what difference does it make if I let him see how badly I need this? "Please."

He doesn't need to be told what I'm pleading for. He knows damn well, and I feel him smiling against my mouth. The tip of one long finger slides breathlessly close to that tiny knot of nerves that's screaming for friction. Just a millimeter more and—

"Jesus, yes." My words come out muffled against his mouth as he strokes me so perfectly I nearly fly off the couch. I clutch at his shoulders like I'm anchoring myself on this couch, on this planet.

Good Lord, Officer Yummy knows how to touch a girl.

I grip his shoulders harder because *ohmygod*, I'm being fingered by a cop. A freakin' officer of the law.

But he's *Austin* right now, sweet and gentle and mind-numbingly sexy Austin, so I give in to the pleasure he's delivering with just the slightest swirl of his fingers. How does he do that?

I'm practically on his lap now with my legs slung over his and my knees splayed open like the lust-addled hussy I am. Self-consciousness seeps into my brain, but Austin pushes it back with the shift of his hand.

I start to protest. "What are you—*Oh*."

Oh, indeed. He dips two fingers inside me as the heel of his hand offers my clit all the delicious friction I'm aching for. The result is the perfect storm of pleasure, thrust and slide, rub and glide, everything a girl could ask for in one massive hand-sized package.

Christ, I'm going to lose it.

He must know, because his free hand tightens around my shoulders, keeping me from falling backward. Between my legs, his fingers keep their steady rhythm, coaxing me closer, tugging me right to the edge. My brain's buzzing with heat but sharply conscious of the fact that his fingers are inside me—*inside me*—for God's sake, is there anything more intimate than that?

There is, and I want it.

But before I can voice the thought, Austin curls his fingers the tiniest bit and hits something really, really good, and I come completely unhinged.

"*Oh!*"

It's the only syllable I can manage before I plunge over the edge, clawing and clutching at his shoulders like I'm either pulling him with me or clinging to him for dear life. Austin doesn't flinch, doesn't miss a beat, even though I'm grabbing him like a crazy woman, like a woman who's never had a guy finger her to orgasm so intensely.

I haven't.

Not like this, anyway, and it's all I can do to hold on to him panting, breathless, delirious, as he brings me back down in one piece.

At least I think I'm in one piece.

As the sensation ebbs, I open my eyes and look around.

"Hi, there." Austin smiles, his blue-gray eyes holding mine. Releasing my shoulders, he lifts his hand to brush a stray curl off my forehead while the other hand slips discreetly from between my thighs.

I slam them together, determined to regain my dignity. "Hello." I clear my throat. "That was—um—thank you."

He laughs, and my heart melts again at the little crinkle at the corner of each eye. "You're welcome. Is this where you get all polite and weird and try to pretend this was some sort of business transaction?"

Heat rises to my face, or maybe it was already there. I feel flushed and discombobulated, and I'm not entirely sure how I ended up here on Austin Dugan's lap.

Sitting on Sergeant Sexypants. Good Lord, it's like a bad '50s pop song.

I swing my legs off his lap so I can plant my feet firmly on the floor. I make a feeble attempt to smooth my skirt down, but it's hopelessly rumpled. I'm halfway between wanting to throw him out of my living room so I can pretend this never happened and wanting to throw him back against the couch cushions, unzip his fly, and straddle that impressive bulge straining at the front of his pants.

"Say something," he says. "You've got a million thoughts running through your head right now, but I'll be damned if I can read a single one of them."

Thank God.

I clear my throat again and wonder if he thinks I've got bronchitis. "Thanks," I say again like some kind of idiot. "That was —nice?"

"Nice?" He laughs and brushes a kiss against my earlobe. "I promise you I can do much better than nice."

My whole body shivers, from the tips of my earlobes to my bare toes curling against the carpet. I make a sound that's somewhere between a gasp and a sob, and somehow find myself clutching at the front of his shirt.

Austin looks down like he's trying to figure out how that happened. I let go and fold my hands into my lap. He reaches down and picks up one of them, then brushes the softest, sweetest kiss across my knuckles.

"But not tonight," he says softly. "Not until you're sure it's what you want."

"I—"

That's all I get out before I stop myself and press my lips together. I'm still not sure if I meant to beg him to stay or ask him to go, but he saves me the trouble by getting to his feet and buttoning up his shirt. He leans down and plants another soft kiss along my hairline.

"You're fucking amazing, Bree Bracelyn," he says. "And I'm going to go now before we end up doing something one of us might regret."

It's not until the door closes behind him that I think to wonder if he meant him or me.

* * *

I LOVE MY BROTHERS.

Sometimes I wish there weren't so damned many of them, but I've never questioned that every single one would cheerfully disembowel someone who hurt me.

But there are some things a girl can't talk about with her brothers, which is why I'm grateful to find myself sitting stiffly on a stool parked at the kitchen island in Jade and Amber King's cozy farmhouse.

I trace a manicured thumbnail over a line in the marbled surface, marveling at the craftsmanship. "Jade and I watched YouTube videos on how to build a concrete countertop," Amber says as she sets a mug of spicy herbal tea in front of me. "It was one of our first big projects when we started remodeling this place."

"You built this?" My opinion of the reindeer ranching, wedding planning sisters has just gone up twelve notches, and it was already pretty high. "And Sean told me you also refinished that old chapel on the edge of your property."

"True story," Jade says as she sets a basket of muffins on the counter and folds a red cloth around them to keep in the heat. "Don't get too impressed, though. The money comes in spurts in this biz, so that's as far as we've gotten until we see how the next season goes."

I swallow back a small bubble of guilt. Sometimes I hate that I have no idea what it's like to struggle financially. I may not have had the best role models of parental warmth and normalcy, but I always knew that the best clothes, the best schools, were just a Visa swipe away.

Maybe that's why I've loved opening Ponderosa Resort with my brothers. Our inheritance may have afforded us a certain financial freedom in building the place, but we've had to be smart about it and work together. We aren't struggling by any means, but we are watching the bottom line.

"Thanks so much for inviting me to brunch," I say now to the King sisters.

"Thank you for including us in the plans with Genevieve Freakin' Dugan." Amber shakes her head in awe. "I still can't believe you talked her into scouting us out for her show."

I sip my tea, grateful for the warmth in my hands and in this small but tidy kitchen. "There's no guarantee she'll do it, but I think I made a strong case for a feature that would spotlight both ends of the country chic wedding spectrum," I say. "You two have the rustic charm, and we've got the luxury pizazz."

"Something for everyone." Jade sips from a big mug with a picture of two reindeer humping, and I suspect my cousin ordered it for her. It seems like something Brandon would buy. "That was nice of Austin to make the introduction."

There it is. My opening. My opportunity to engage in the sort of girl talk I dreamed of when I was an awkward teen with no idea how these things worked. I swallow back a mouthful of tea and consider how to phrase my next line.

"You two know Austin well?"

Amber gives a knowing smile, and I suspect I've just stepped through the secret passageway into the girl-talk zone. It's nice here, and the tea is tasty. "Jade knows him better than I do, since he and Brandon were buddies in high school," she says. "But all of us ended up back in Central Oregon after college, so I guess we're part of the same club."

There's a pang in my chest that fills me with an achy brand of middle school nostalgia, but I force it back with another swallow of tea. "He's a good guy, then?"

"A *great* guy," Amber says. "Three years ago, he worked this case where a girl got kidnapped over in Portland, but the bad guy brought her through here on his way to California."

Jade picks up the thread of the story and runs with it. "Cops in six counties were after the guy, and a lot of them were chasing their tails. It was Austin who thought to dig into the suspect's background to discover the guy had an ex-girlfriend out in Prineville. Then he tracked down the ex's brother, and then the brother's best friend, and eventually found the guy sleeping in a barn with his victim handcuffed to him."

"Wow," I say, simultaneously impressed and uneasy. "He sounds…thorough."

"He is." Amber grins. "But something tells me you're interested in more than his cop skills."

"True story." I'm echoing Jade's words earlier, something I read about once in a book on making friends and forging relationships.

I'd like to pretend it was part of my curriculum for public relations professionals, but I read it when I was fifteen and friendless and desperately wishing to connect with *someone*. Anyone.

Something about the way Jade studies me over the rim of her mug tells me she knows what I'm wondering about. There's a telepathic connection between women who had trouble fitting in as girls, and I sensed it the first day I met Jade.

"He wasn't one of the bullies," she says softly. "If that's what you're wondering. Austin was never one of the guys who made my life hell in school."

"I'm glad." Gladder than she probably realizes, though I suppose I could have guessed this about Austin. "So why hasn't one of the local girls snapped him up?"

"They've tried," Amber says. "He's dated quite a bit and even seemed serious for a few months with Chelsea from the cupcake shop."

"This was before she had the baby," Jade says. "Don't worry, he's not the daddy. The kid's father is long gone."

"Chelsea is a single mom?" I file this information in the back of my head, curious how I never heard this before. I'm usually pretty astute with my info gathering.

"It's one of those scandals locals don't gossip about much since it involves a kid," Amber says. "Small town folks are chatty, but we draw the line somewhere."

I'm dying to ask more but figure I'm better off respecting the rule about avoiding kid-related gossip. Besides, I'm more interested in Austin.

Leave it to Jade to read my mind. "So are you still committed to your no-cops dating rule, or are you softening on that?" she asks.

"And what is it with the rule, anyway?" Amber pipes up before I can answer the first question. "If you don't mind me asking."

I do mind a little. But I can't show up here hoping to bond with potential girlfriends and not share at least a little bit about myself. I don't need to read friend-making manuals to know that. "It's just a personality thing, I guess."

There, that's something.

It's true, too, though the sisters' faces suggest they're expecting more. I spin my mug on the counter and try to come up with more. "You know how sometimes you just don't mesh with certain kinds of people?"

Amber lifts an eyebrow. "I'm no expert, but you seem to be meshing just fine with Austin," she says. "*Meshing* being a euphemism for—"

"I know what you mean," Jade says, slugging her sister in the shoulder before Amber can finish that thought. "Brandon's a Marine. He works for the recruitment center now, but he was still active duty when we got together. There's a certain personality that goes with that, and I wasn't sure I could handle that."

"You're handling it pretty well now." Amber's still smirking, but at least it's directed at Jade now. "But you like a guy who's all rigid and alpha," she says. "Maybe that's not Bree's thing."

"Oh, it is." The words slip out in a wispy, high voice I barely recognize as my own. I'm picturing Austin's fingers between my legs, his touch commanding and in charge.

God, that was hot.

"Now we're making you blush." Jade shakes her head at Amber and shoves a plate of bacon at her. "Put this on the table. We're just about ready to eat."

Amber rolls her eyes but takes the platter and trudges obediently to the dining room table. Jade watches her for a second, then looks at me and lowers her voice.

"She's bad with the teasing sometimes, but I hope you know you can come to us with anything," she murmurs. "Either of us, anytime. If you need to talk."

I swallow hard, surprised by the swell of emotion bubbling up my throat. "Thank you," I whisper, digging my fingernails into my knee under the bar. "I appreciate that."

More than she knows.

But the fact that there's still a whole lot she doesn't know has me pressing my lips together, hoping I don't slip and say too much.

Amber returns to the kitchen and grabs the basket of muffins off the counter. "Seriously, though, Austin's a great guy," she says. "Kind to kids and animals, smart as hell, really driven career-wise. Do you know how rare it is to be a contender for police chief at his age?"

I shake my head, even though I Googled this the other night. An ambitious cop would normally follow the path from police academy to patrol officer and through the ranks from sergeant to middle management positions like lieutenant and then captain. But Austin's advanced degree, along with the fact that he's racked up every award and accolade in the books, has put him on the fast track to being the big man in charge.

Despite my cop aversion, that's kind of a turn-on.

Amber brushes past me, her dark hair brushing my arm. "From what I hear, he's pretty much a shoo-in as chief as long as he doesn't do anything dumb in the next year or two."

Jade laughs and scoops up a basket of muffins. "Like that's an issue," she says. "The guy keeps his nose so clean it glows. He could lead a sleigh team of reindeer on a foggy night."

Amber rolls her eyes. "Spoken like a lunatic reindeer rancher."

I force a smile, even though something inside me just crumpled into a tight paper ball and combusted. What the hell am I doing thinking I could start something with a guy like Austin? A guy with a bright future and a moral compass so strong it's practically a force of nature.

I can't screw that up for him.

I need to just keep my hands to myself and all my stupid skeletons crammed tight in the closet where they belong. Where they can't harm anyone, especially Austin.

As I stand up and make my way to the table, I say a little prayer I'm strong enough to do that.

CHAPTER 9

AUSTIN

*J*t's been two days since I've heard from Bree. Two days since I felt her breath on my neck and watched her eyes darken with yearning. Two days since I felt her clenching slick and tight around my fingers.

I know I should play it cool. A smart guy wouldn't text more than twice or leave more than one voicemail saying as casually as possible what a great time he had and that he's hoping to do it again.

But I'm not cool or even all that smart, which is how I find myself volunteering to drive Aunt Gen out to Ponderosa Ranch on Monday afternoon for her meeting with Bree.

"It really is breathtaking, isn't it?" Gen says.

I'm still thinking about Bree, so I start nodding before I realize she's looking at the mountains. "The views are great," I say. "They went to a lot of trouble to make sure all the dining tables are angled so everyone gets the mountain view eye candy."

She looks at me like she knows I was totally quoting Bree, but she refrains from commenting. Instead, she pulls out her phone and clicks off a couple pictures of the massive Ponderosa Luxury

Ranch Resort sign with the resort logo spelled out in cast iron curlicue.

"The attention to detail is exquisite," she says. "I can think of at least three clients who'd swoon over the chance to have that kind of backdrop in their wedding photos."

"Beautiful," I agree, distracted again. Bree steps out onto the paver walkway in front of the lodge. She's wearing a fitted gray skirt and a red shirt that's drapey and soft and shows just the faintest hint of the curves hidden beneath.

I've had my hands on those.

The idea flits through my head with a chest-thumping pride, but I push it aside as I pull into a parking space. Bree strides toward my truck, barely hiding the flash of alarm in her eyes when she realizes I've accompanied Aunt Gen.

"Don't worry," I assure her as I swing myself out of the truck. "I promise I'm not crashing your meeting. Just taking you up on your offer."

"Offer?"

I open the door to let Virginia come bounding out. Bree's face lights up with joy, and I feel only slightly guilty about using my dog to warm the heart of a woman who seems less than excited about seeing me.

"Oh," she says, stooping down to scratch Virginia's ears. "You're here to test-drive the dog park. It's nice to see you again, good girl!"

"It's lovely to see you again, too, dear." Genevieve gives Bree a wry wink as she walks around the truck to stand beside her. "You weren't exaggerating one bit. It's absolutely stunning out here."

"I'm excited to give you a tour." Bree stands and smooths her hands down the front of her skirt. "Would you like to start with the spa?"

"Whatever you think is best."

"Let's get some fresh cucumber water or maybe a glass of

champagne so we have something to drink while we make the rounds."

The two of them disappear into the lodge, leaving Virginia and me standing at the edge of the parking area. I glance down to see my dog looking vaguely disappointed. "You and me both, girl."

"Dog park's that way."

The gruff voice comes from behind, and I pivot to see Mark standing at the edge of the lodge. How much of that did he just see?

"Doing some wood cutting?" I manage as Mark stands there looking vaguely menacing with an axe.

He doesn't respond, which means axe murdering isn't out of the question. He doesn't smile or say anything but does give a low grunt. "That's a good lookin' dog you've got there."

"Thanks. She's part coyote."

Mark leans the axe against the lodge, then bends to scratch her ears. I try to think of something else to say. "Thanks for putting out Bree's fire the other night. She felt awful about leaving that candle."

"We all have shitty judgment sometimes."

He's looking at the dog and not me, but I sense there's more to that remark than idle chit-chat.

"True enough," I agree. "Let he who's never been a dumbass cast the first stone."

He straightens up and looks me dead in the eye. "Isn't that sort of your job, though? Casting stones?"

"Not really." I try not to let my surprise show as I consider the odd turn in conversation. "I'm a cop, not a judge. I enforce the laws, but I don't make them. Or even question them."

Mark says nothing to that, but the intensity of his expression has me wanting to look away. I don't, though. It's not my first time staring down a guy who's sizing me up. Or who's intent on making me blink first, which I absolutely won't do.

Virginia barks sharply, and we break eye contact at the same time.

"Look, Mark," I say. "I know you're protective of your sister. I've got sisters, too, so I know how it is."

"You do." It's halfway between a question and a statement, and I wonder if he's testing me.

"I know no one's ever good enough for them, and God knows I've tried to run off plenty of guys I thought didn't have their best interest at heart," I say. "I just want you to know my intentions are good. I like Bree. I like her a lot, and I want to keep getting to know her."

He studies me for a long time, and I try to avoid looking like a guy who had a hand up Bree's skirt forty-eight hours ago. Finally, Mark nods like he's just run a scan on my brainwaves and made a determination. God knows what it is.

"There's a basket of tennis balls next to the dog park gate," he says. "Help yourself."

He turns and walks away.

* * *

"I'LL EMAIL you a couple of custom menus to give you a sense of what we can do." Sean Bracelyn—Bree's famous chef brother—is talking to Aunt Gen in front of the lodge when I stroll up with a tired dog on my heels.

Sean looks up and waves, and my aunt follows suit. "Austin, I was wondering where you'd disappeared to," she says. "This place is amazing."

"Wait 'til you see the reindeer ranch next door." Sean grins. "Not that I'm an unbiased party, but I think it'll give you a cool look at the other side of the coin."

Aunt Gen smiles back, picking up on the hint of a love story. Her favorite thing, which is what makes her TV show so popular.

"That's right, Bree mentioned you're engaged to one of the sisters," Genevieve says. "Amber, right?"

"Not engaged." Sean smiles. "Yet." The guy looks downright ecstatic, and I can't help liking him. He's clearly nuts about the pretty brunette next door, and it's cool that he wears it on his sleeve.

"I'm visiting Amber's ranch next," Gen says. "I can't wait to meet her."

"I'm happy to drive you if you want." Sean looks at me. "I'm headed there anyway to see Amber. It's no trouble at all."

"I accept," Gen says before I can open my mouth. My aunt pats me on the cheek like I'm six years old, even though she has to stretch up to do it. "Go see that girl of yours. Bree's in her office."

She wanders off with Sean before I can say anything about Bree not being my girl. Not officially, anyway. Or did she say something else to Gen? The thought makes my dumb heart swell, even though I know it's not true. The fact that she hasn't returned my calls seems like a good indication of where her head is at, though I can't help thinking about where my hand was just a few nights ago. Didn't that mean something?

I glance down at my dog like she might have the answers. Virginia looks at me and yawns, then curls into a donut shape next to the big water feature beside the front door.

"Stay right here, girl," I tell her unnecessarily. It would take a backhoe to move her from this cozy nap spot.

I wipe the tennis ball dust onto my jeans and head through the massive doors of the lodge. Turning left at the lobby, I move toward Bree's office. I hesitate when I hear her voice.

"We've got them doing the couples' massage class tomorrow morning at our day spa," she's saying. "I'll see about getting them out on a few day trips. I've heard about some hot springs that aren't too far from here. Maybe some hikes or something."

There's some more murmuring, and I wonder if I should

retreat back to the lobby to wait for her there instead of eaves-dropping like a creeper. But then she's saying her goodbyes, and I hear the clatter of her phone on her desk.

"You can come in, Austin."

I move toward her door, wondering if she sensed my presence or something cheesy like that.

She stands and points to the wall beside the door. "Mirror," she says with a smile. "Mark put it up after I complained I couldn't see who was hanging around in the lobby."

Her smile makes my chest feel like someone's set off one of those fizzy bath bombs my sisters always buy each other for Christmas, and yes, I did try the one they gave me last year. "How'd things go with my aunt?"

"Great." Bree stays standing, so I do the same, wondering if she wants to make a hasty exit. "She seemed really excited about the ballroom, which is perfect for huge, formal events," she continues. "Sean did a little taste test for her with some of his best wedding food, and she seemed to really like that."

"I'm not surprised," I tell her. "The stuff you served at the grand opening was incredible."

"I'll tell him you said so." Her green eyes are flashing, and I love seeing her this excited. "I don't want to count my chickens too soon or anything, but I'm hopeful," she says. "Genevieve thinks it would make a great segment for the week they're devoting to Pacific Northwest wedding venues."

"That's awesome. Congratulations."

"Thanks." Bree clasps her hands in front of her like a kid who's been told not to grab anything in the candy store. "And thanks for introducing me to her." She nibbles the edge of her lip, and I wonder what's on her mind.

I don't have to wonder long.

"Thanks for uh—the other night." She looks down at her hands, and her cheeks get another shade pinker. Magenta or fuchsia or whatever the hell you call that pretty shade of dark pink.

It's all I can do to stop myself from reaching for her. "You don't have to thank me. Touching you wasn't exactly community service."

She looks up, and my breath catches in my throat. Maybe I shouldn't have said that. Sounded too eager or whatever.

"I didn't mean for that to happen," she says slowly. "But I'm glad it did."

Wait, what?

"Really?"

The smile she gives me is oddly shy. "I know I shouldn't be, and I was all set to tell you we probably shouldn't do it again," she says. "But then you show up in that blue shirt that matches your eyes, and you've got your adorable dog and your sweet aunt, and you're doing the whole Officer Velvet Voice thing, and the next thing I know—"

"Officer Velvet Voice?"

"Right," she says, biting her lip again. "It's your normal voice, I guess. It's sort of irresistible."

"Thanks. I think." I still can't figure out what's going on here.

"I know I've been giving you sort of mixed signals, but I'm figuring this stuff out as I go along." She gives me a shaky smile and tucks a curl behind one ear. "I'm hot for you. Obviously. But I'm not quite sure what to do about it."

This vulnerable side to Bree, it's something I haven't seen before. It's ridiculously sexy, and I'm fighting like hell to keep from reaching for her. "So can I see you again sometime?"

She sighs, and the look that flits across her face looks like genuine remorse. "I'm not sure that's going to work right now."

Disappointment drags my heart down like an anchor. "Is it because of the cop thing or something else?"

"Neither, exactly." She sighs and gestures toward her phone. "I know it sounds like an excuse, but I'm kind of freaking out about work stuff right now."

"What's wrong?" Maybe I can help.

She shakes her head and knocks over her pen cup. I start to reach for it, but she's already scooping them back into place. "I've got all these travel journalists here right now, which should be a good thing," she says. "But nothing's going the way it's supposed to."

"The FAM tours, right." Do I get bonus points for remembering what they're called? I lean against her wall, careful not to bump the mirror. "What's going on?"

Bree's eyes flick across my chest then back to my face. It's so fast I almost missed it, and my ego swells just a little. "I have three couples here as part of a FAM trip that's all about romance and couples' travel," she says. "That's their schtick—they all write about traveling as a pair."

I nod so she knows I'm listening. "One of them is your college buddy and his husband."

She smiles, and I can tell I've scored brownie points for remembering. "That's right. You were paying attention."

She sounds amazed, like it's not a given I'd be hanging on her every word. "That's Donovan and Sam, and they run the Nomadic Dudes travel site," she says. "I guess they ran into some homophobic crap at the Dandelion Café yesterday, which sucks from more than just a PR standpoint. He's my best friend, and I hate that they have to deal with hurtful comments. Everyone in town is normally so nice."

I hate it even more than she does, since there's a good chance I know whoever's responsible. It's a small town, and that's my regular breakfast spot. "Who was it? Not one of the servers?"

"No, just a customer," she says. "I wrote the name down somewhere. Anyway, that's only one of the things falling apart right now." She glances at the door, then leans across me and pushes it shut. It's everything I can do not to respond when her breast brushes my arm on the way back.

"There's some drama with the other two couples," she says, lowering her voice. "Chris and Shawna are with the Wandering Hearts travel blog. Sweet couple—he's Australian, and I think she's from California. Apparently, there's some tension with the other duo."

"Tension like fighting over pizza deliveries?"

"No, the opposite." She grimaces, and I try to imagine what the opposite of a pizza fight might be. "Graham and Gigi—that's the other couple, from the Lovebird Journeys travel site—they've got a reputation for having more of an *open relationship*."

I study Bree's face as her cheeks flush with color and she glances down at her hands, suddenly very interested in her manicure.

"You mean they're swingers? Wife swapping or whatever?"

She winces. "That's the rumor. Anyway, Gigi is this sleek, beautiful Instagram blonde who's always posting provocative photos. Stuff like 'oh, here I am looking out over this lush mountain vista and, oops, I forgot my pants.'"

I'm not on social media much, but I think I get the gist of what she's talking about. "My sister, Meredith, is on Instagram. She shows me stuff like that sometimes. Women who are all, 'Doesn't everyone lounge in the backyard hammock wearing nothing but a thong?'"

"Exactly," Bree says. "Or last night it was, 'I've forgotten how to eat ice cream, so I'll just deep-throat the cone.'"

My brain swerves a little at the deep-throat reference, but I force myself to stay on track. "So you're worried about her covering her naked body with honey and posing by your pool or something?"

"That, too, but I'm more worried about the other couple—Chris and Shawna?" She shakes her head, and a curl flops over her forehead. "One of my brothers saw Gigi alone with Chris in the game room last night. I guess he looked a little too enthusiastic about teaching her to play pool."

"Yikes." I may know nothing about Instagram, but even I can guess how this could lead to bad publicity. It only takes one pissed off blogger and a viral post to ruin the reputation of a new business like Bree's. "You don't think Chris's girlfriend is in on it? Like maybe they're swingers, too?"

"Shawna?" Bree shakes her head. "No. I had breakfast with her this morning. She seemed aware of Gigi's reputation, but convinced Chris would never act on it. I can't say anything because I don't know if something's happened yet, but I feel an obligation to make sure nothing does happen. I don't want anyone getting hurt."

I can't imagine having to deal with this sort of PR crap. Supervising deputies and chasing down bad guys is more my speed, but managing a bunch of horny millennials with a habit of posting every meal, every bodily function online would make me want to hide under a rock. "What can you do?"

Bree bites her lip. "I'm thinking maybe I can send each couple out on some excursions, little day trips that get them away from each other."

"Ah, the hot springs." I just admitted to eavesdropping on her phone call, but Bree doesn't seem bothered. "That's a good one. Or Crater Lake. The Painted Hills are nice, or Smith Rock."

"These are great, keep them coming." She turns and scribbles on a notepad beside her phone. "Gigi and Graham have this whole series they do about hot springs around the world, so maybe you could tell me more about that one you mentioned. The place where you found Virginia?"

"Summer Lake Hot Springs." I like where this is going. "You want me to take you out there to see it?"

She blows a curl off her forehead, and I try not to fixate on her mouth. "Would you mind?" she asks. "I don't want to send them there if I haven't seen it myself, but I thought—"

"Done," I say. "Your timing's perfect. I'm actually off for the next two days."

Bree looks up at me with a question in her eyes. "You said it's just a day trip?"

I'm not sure what the right answer is here, so I play it safe. "It can be if you get an early start and don't mind coming back in the dark. Or there are cabins and tent sites you can rent. Totally up to you."

She nods, looking thoughtful. She hesitates, like she's considering something a lot bigger than a road trip. Like the weight of the world is on her shoulders.

"I'd like that," she says slowly. "I'd like to spend the night."

I study her face, trying to read between the lines. She didn't say "spend the night with you," and maybe I'm a presumptuous prick for thinking what I am.

But I can't help going there, can't help picturing her beneath me or hearing those soft little sounds she made the other night as she came apart in my arms.

"Do you want to camp, or should I check into cabins? They've got one bedroom, two bedroom—"

"Maybe camping." She bites her lip, a flicker of uncertainty in her eyes. "I've never done it before."

"I'll see if I can get a campsite reservation," I offer. "If you're up for that."

"I'm up for it," she says slowly, squaring her shoulders like she's just decided something. "I'm ready to try something new."

CHAPTER 10

BREE

$\mathcal{M}$y whole adult life, I've been a fixer. I doled out tough love and maraschino cherries when Brandon hit a rough patch with Jade. When things blew up with Sean's hot mess of a mother, I gave him warm tea and a soft spot to land.

But I've never been on the receiving end of it. Sure, my father swooped in with a checkbook now and then, but most things can't be fixed with money.

That's why it feels so good to see Austin in action right now. It's the first time anyone's taken charge of some catastrophe in my life and said, "I've got this" without hesitation or financial agenda.

If I had any hope of resisting my feelings for him, it vanished with those three words.

"This won't take long." He's steering the truck with one hand as Virginia pants happily at the window, her breath fogging the glass. "Bob Mosely's ranch is just off the highway as we're headed south."

"Are you sure we should do this?" I fiddle with the zipper on my jacket and hope I haven't made a mistake in telling him what happened to Donovan and Sam at the Dandelion Café. Maybe I should have left things alone.

"I want to handle this," he says. "It's the least I can do. Besides, I know the guy. My dad and I go hunting with him every fall."

"Maybe it's not a big deal," I murmur. "I'm still new in town. Maybe I shouldn't start pissing off the good ol' boys club or—"

"It *is* a big deal," he says. "This is my hometown, and it matters to me how people are treated here." He reaches across the seat and rests a reassuring hand on mine. "Leave the good ol' boys to me. I know how to handle them."

I'm jumping out of my skin, but Austin's posture is relaxed and easy. He's driving like a guy who grew up navigating these desolate country roads in his sleep. In all my public relations courses, this wasn't something I learned. I understand crisis management in a corporate setting, but not like this. Not when it involves my best friend and a grumpy rancher.

But I trust Austin to know small town politics better than I do. "Okay."

"You can wait in the truck if you want."

"No, I want to be there," I say. "This involves my business. My *friends*."

It takes us less than five minutes to turn off the highway and wind our way along a gravel road that leads to Bob's ranch. Two spotted farm dogs come trotting out, barking their heads off. Virginia sits up and growls beside me.

"Stay here, girl," he says. "We'll be back in a minute."

Austin leaves the windows cracked for her as he gets out. I'm grateful he's driving his truck today instead of the Volvo or even a cop car. I know he said the truck does best on the dirt roads we'll be traveling, but I can't help thinking there's another reason. If optics are everything, it helps that Austin kinda looks like a good ol' boy right now. He saunters up the walkway and my girl parts do a pleasant squeeze. Apparently, they've got a thing for the badass, superhero side of Austin.

He strides up the walkway like he's on duty, and I can almost see the gun clipped to a heavy utility belt around his waist. It isn't there, but he moves like it is. Austin Dugan makes jeans and a baseball cap look like a cop uniform.

"Morning, Bob." Austin touches the bill of his hat as a gray-haired man ambles out onto his front porch.

The guy wears cowboy boots and worn jeans with creases ironed at the front, and he's holding a blue and white enamel mug. His gaze flicks to me, and I manage a small wave before he turns back to Austin.

"Howdy, son." He adjusts the brim of his hat. "Heard about the promotion. What can I do you for?"

I've never understood that bizarre turn of phrase, *what can I do you for,* but I keep my happy PR smile pasted in place as Austin grips the guy's hand in a firm shake.

"Have you met Bree Bracelyn?" He gestures to me, and that's my cue to step up and extend a hand.

"Pleasure to meet you," I say. "My brothers and I own Ponderosa Ranch."

I deliberately leave out the "Luxury Resort" part of the name, figuring that might earn me some points. It's the same reason I mentioned my brothers. I might be new to small-town life, but I'm not new to classism or sexist viewpoints.

Or to homophobia, which is why we're here this morning.

"Pleasure to meet you, ma'am," Bob says, and I wonder if he knows the reason we're standing on his front porch. "You've got everyone gabbing about that place."

"That's actually what we want to talk to you about." Austin's tone is friendly and even, but there's an edge to it now. I wonder if Bob hears it. "I understand you ran into a couple of resort guests at the Dandelion the other day. Travel writers Bree's been working with."

Bob frowns. "The two fruits?"

Austin doesn't react to the slur, but I feel him tense beside me. His body's still loose and casual, but there's a coiled-spring energy radiating off him now. "They're journalists with a huge international following," Austin says. "And they're friends of Bree's."

I nod and keep my mouth shut. Austin is handling this, and I trust him to know the best way to do it.

Bob scrubs a hand over his chin, his brow still furrowed. "Couple'a fellows together like that," he says. "Just walking around like it's no big deal."

"Actually, it isn't." Austin's tone is all velvet-voice cool, but his jaw is rigid. "They travel all over the world writing about places that are friendly to visitors. *All kinds* of visitors, towns like ours." He clears his throat and looks Bob dead square in the face, blue eyes unblinking. "Only it sounds like you might have said some things to make them feel unwelcome."

The tips of Bob's ears go red, and he kicks his boot through a cluster of dried weeds on the porch. "Aw, we were just joking around."

My blood starts to simmer, but Austin reaches for my hand. I'm not sure if it's a signal to me or to Bob, but one thing's clear—Austin is in charge here.

"Doesn't sound like the guests found it all that funny," he says. "Is it true you made crude comments about someone else's sex life in a café filled with kids?"

Bob's ears get redder, and I can't tell if he's angry or embarrassed. "I just asked 'em who was the guy and who was the girl," he grumbles.

I can't bite my tongue this time. "I believe the way you phrased it was 'who does the fudge packing and who gets his fudge packed?'"

"Bob," Austin says, giving my fingers a supportive squeeze. "I'm gonna go out on a limb here and say you wouldn't like it much if you and Lucinda walked into the Dandelion and someone asked about whether the two of you like getting freaky with whips and a horse bridle."

Bob's face turns the same tomato red as his ears, and he sputters a little before answering. "But that's no one's business but—"

"Exactly." Austin's still smiling as he cuts him off, and I realize this is his version of cheerfully-angry. It's a skill I wish I possessed. "What people do behind closed doors is none of anyone else's business, and it's sure as hell not something to talk about in front of women and kids, is it?"

Bob doesn't answer at first, but he does an infinitesimal little head shake. "It's not right," he mutters.

I don't know if he's talking about sex in general, or just gay people, but maybe it doesn't matter. "It's not our place to judge, is it?" Austin's voice is so good-natured it's like they're talking about crops or the latest golf scores, but the sharp edge to it makes me glad he's on my team. That he's standing up for me, for my business, my friends.

"It's up to us to treat people with kindness," Austin continues, scratching one of Bob's dogs behind the ears. "Newcomers, old-timers, visitors—we treat 'em all with respect so our kids learn that from us. You're the one who told me that, remember?"

"Yeah," Bob mutters. "But I didn't mean—"

"Everyone," Austin interrupts, and this time there's no mistaking the steel in his voice. "In this town, we don't bully people. We don't throw stones, and we sure as hell don't go out of our way to publicly embarrass people about their sex lives. You hear what I'm saying?"

I get the sense there's more to this conversation than I realize. That theory solidifies as Bob winces, then gives a grudging nod.

"Sure," he grunts. "Whatever you say."

"Good." Austin claps the other man on the shoulder in a gesture that looks downright brotherly. "We still on for the elk hunting in a few weeks?"

"Yeah," Bob says, not meeting Austin's eyes. "Your dad said he got a new jerky gun?"

I have no idea what a jerky gun is, but this is why Austin is so good at this. He speaks the language in a way I can't. I don't know how he pulled it off, but Austin has somehow managed to speak to this guy with both respect and authority, mixing in a tiny bit of humor and intimidation while he's at it. I'm in awe.

And a little turned on, if I'm being honest.

"I'll give you a call about target shooting next week," Austin's saying, and I realize I may have missed part of the conversation, while mentally undressing the cop. "Good seeing you, Bob."

"You, too." Bob touches the brim of his cowboy hat, and I almost wish I had a hat of my own to return the gesture. "Nice meeting you, ma'am."

"You, too."

I wait until we're back in the car and halfway down the driveway to throw my arms around Austin's neck. "Oh my God, that was amazing."

He looks at me and smiles. "Aren't you supposed to be buckled up?"

I flutter my lashes and plant a kiss beside his ear before planting my butt back in the seat. "Are you going to arrest me if I don't obey the seatbelt law?"

"Maybe," he says, both hands on the wheel as he heads back out onto the highway. "I do have a pair of handcuffs in back."

I know we're both teasing, but I do one of those full-body sex shivers as I clip my seatbelt into place and fold my hands in my lap to keep myself from groping Lieutenant Luscious. "Seriously, that was incredible," I tell him. "I can't believe how well you handled that. You sure you don't have a degree in public relations?"

He laughs and slides on a pair of sunglasses that make him look ten times hotter, if that's even possible. "Nope. Just a degree in criminal justice, a little small-town sensibility, and a lifetime of memorizing everyone else's secrets."

A cold trickle of ice slides through my veins, but I keep my smile in place. "What do you mean?"

"Police dispatch notes are public records," Austin says. "Let's just say my comment about the horse bridle wasn't pulled out of thin air."

Oh. And holy shit.

I stare at Austin with new respect, not sure if I'm more impressed or fearful about the realization that I'm driving a hundred miles into the middle of nowhere with a guy so skilled at using someone's dirty laundry against them.

I know I should be careful. I know there are a million reasons to keep my heart and my hands away from Austin Dugan. But I can't help sliding my palm over the smooth muscles of his thigh, curling my fingers around all that coiled heat. "Thank you," I say. "I owe you for that."

"You don't owe me anything," he says. "Just doing my job."

And there it is, that reminder of who Austin is. What he does for a living, and how it's a part of him no matter how close we get.

I take a deep breath and will myself to remember that.

* * *

"Grab the pole and slide it in nice and slow."

I confess I've spent several nights with my hand in my pajama pants imagining Austin Dugan murmuring something like that in my ear.

But this isn't how I pictured it.

"There you go," he says as I guide the tent pole through the little sleeve thingy and out the other end. "This is really your first time camping?"

"Yes," I admit, sticking the little peg thingy into the hole on the end of the pole the way Austin showed me earlier. I should probably learn some terminology that doesn't involve the word *thingy.*

I blow a curl off my forehead and wonder if I should have dressed more casually. I got the jeans down okay, but I hope he can't tell these boots are the designer variety instead of something more practical.

"My dad took my brothers camping when it was their turn to visit him," I continue. "But I got horseback riding and spa appointments instead."

"Huh," Austin says. "That's something, I guess."

Shit, did I sound like poor little rich girl again? "I'm not complaining," I assure him. "But I wouldn't have minded sleeping outside. Or learning to fish or use power tools or all the other things my brothers were coached on before they could even drive."

Austin grins and finishes pounding one of the tent stakes into the ground. His shoulders bunch as he brings the hammer down, and I wonder why I never dated an outdoorsy guy before. Or a cop.

Okay, I know why I didn't date cops.

"You know how to make a campfire?" he asks as he stands up, brushing his hands on his jeans.

"That I can handle." I don't tell him I spent hours poring over YouTube videos to figure it out so I could show guests at the resort how to run their fancy fire pits.

We set to work building the fire together, crumpling paper and adding bits of kindling until the flames start to grow. We work well together, and I can't help wondering what it would be like to do this sort of thing all the time.

"I think I would have liked learning this stuff as a kid," I admit. "Learning how to make fire instead of how to distinguish a fish fork from a dessert fork."

"There's a special fork for fish?"

"Absolutely." A twinge of self-consciousness needles me, but Austin's not looking at me like he's judging. He seems genuinely curious. "There are salad forks and dinner forks and deli forks and fruit forks and ice cream forks."

He snorts and arranges a log on the pile of glowing embers. "Rich people eat ice cream with a fork?"

"I guess it's sort of like a spork," I say, surprised to discover I'm not bristling at all about the 'rich people' comment. There's no snideness in Austin's voice, no trace of nastiness at all. Just curiosity. "You're supposed to use the tines to break apart the ice cream before you spoon it into your mouth."

"And to think I've been missing out on these special fork experiences." He grins. "I had no idea."

I should probably drop the whole fork issue, but Austin seems genuinely intrigued. Today's visit with Bob gave me a glimpse of the inner workings of his world. I suppose I can offer a small glimpse of mine.

"There are even special forks just for oysters," I admit.

"Let me guess—they've got a built-in shell cracker or something?"

"Not quite," I say. "They're about four inches long and they have three curved tines that follow the shape of the shell."

Austin laughs and shakes his head. "I learn something new every day."

"I have a ridiculously-huge collection of flatware I got from my mother," I tell him. "I don't know why I still have it, but you can call me anytime you want a fork."

Shit. Did that sound filthy? I didn't mean for it to, but the way Austin's looking at me suggests the same dirty thought just fluttered through his brain. Is it wrong that I kinda want him to say it?

Instead, he sits back on his heels and smiles. "I didn't bring any fancy forks, but I do have hobo bundles in the cooler."

"If that's something to eat, I might love you. I totally forgot about food."

A look of intense hunger moves across his face, and I wonder if he's thinking about more than campfire chow. "I thought we'd make dinner first and wait for the sun to go down," he says. "Then we can check out the hot springs."

"When it's dark?" I glance toward the rustic timber and corrugated-metal building and wonder if it's lame to ask about wild animals lurking around here.

Virginia Woof must sense my uncertainty because she stands up from her spot next to the cooler and ambles over to nudge my hand with her nose. I stroke her soft ears, which soothes me instantly. "Are the hot springs inside or outside?"

"Both," Austin says. "There's a bigger pool in that barn-looking structure, but I like the smaller ones outside. I thought it would be nice to have your first time be under the stars."

A shudder of excitement runs through me before my brain catches up and reminds me he's talking about my first time soaking in a hot spring.

Or is he? Maybe the fact that I agreed to an overnight stay makes it a foregone conclusion we're going to sleep together. Or maybe not. He did bring two sleeping bags. He's arranging them in the tent now, along with some sort of inflatable camping pad. I resist the urge to peer inside to see how close he's positioning them to one another.

On top of each other might be nice.

"I'll grab the food," I tell him, conscious of the heat in my cheeks. I open the cooler and let the chilled air cool my face. "What do hobo bundles look like, exactly?"

"They're foil packets filled with peppers and onions and sliced up sausage, plus some herbs and secret sauce," Austin calls from inside the tent. "My dad's special recipe."

"You and your dad seem pretty close?"

"For sure." He emerges through the door flap and turns to zip it shut. Then he joins me beside the fire, settling into one of the camp chairs he brought.

Camp chairs, that's a thing. I can't believe how much *stuff* is involved in an activity that's basically just sleeping outside. Or maybe Austin's trying to ease me in gradually by bringing all these accoutrements from home.

"He's a good guy, my dad," Austin says. "A little old-school, but he taught me everything I know about law enforcement and life and—well, everything."

"I envy you." I offer a small smile, so he knows I'm not crazy-jealous, but I see concern in his eyes anyway. "I know my dad loved me, in his own way," I continue, pushing past his pity. "And my mom is—well, my mom."

"You see her much?"

"Not a lot," I admit. "She still hasn't seen the resort. She's been busy."

"What does she do?"

"For work?" I laugh at the idea of my mother having a job. "She marries rich men with commitment issues, then takes them to the cleaners when they cheat."

"Seriously?"

I nod as Austin arranges the foil packets in the fire. "Sometimes I think she only had me so she could milk the extra money out of my father," I admit. "A little child support to go with the alimony."

"Huh." He doesn't say anything else, and I remember his words to Bob.

It's not our place to judge, is it?

Maybe not, but I can tell Austin is mystified by my upbringing.

"I love my mother," I say. "I do. But honestly, we never had a chance to be close. I was at boarding school for most of the year, and summer camps when school wasn't in session. I could probably count on one hand the number of nights my mother and I spent under the same roof after I turned five."

"That's so crazy to me," he says. "No offense. It's just a lot different from how I grew up."

"Most of my brothers were raised the same way I was," I say. "Not Mark, but Sean and James and Jonathan and—"

"How many brothers do you have again?"

"A lot. Way more than you've met." I frown. "Probably more than I've met."

"I can't believe you turned out so normal."

"You think I'm normal?" I grin like he's just told me I'm pretty. "That might be the nicest thing anyone's ever said to me."

Austin laughs and nudges the foil bundles with a long stick. "Relatively speaking."

I lean back in my camp chair and look out at the horizon. The sun is sinking low into a nest of pink and orange clouds while crickets sing songs about it from somewhere in the wavy brown field to our right. Virginia rolls onto her side and sighs.

"I don't mean to sound ungrateful," I tell Austin. "I grew up with a lot of privilege, and I know that."

He looks up and his blue-gray eyes search mine. "Did you have close friends there?"

"Where?"

"Boarding school. I guess I'm picturing it like in the movies where there are all these little cliques and clubs and stuff. Just wondering where you fit in."

I swallow hard and remind myself this is an innocent question. He's just curious about a world that's as unfamiliar to him as camp chairs and hobo bundles are to me.

"It was—challenging, socially." There's the understatement of the year.

"I see."

That's what I'm afraid of. That he really does see, that he knows all my secrets. That he'll find out what I've done.

"It got better in college," I tell him, desperate to fill the silence. "That's where I learned some social skills, started figuring out who I was and where I fit into the world."

"You seem like you've nailed it now." He smiles and pokes at the foil-wrapped bundles with a stick. "How old were you when you graduated?"

"From college?" I nibble the edge of my lip and wonder why he's asking. "Twenty-three when I finished undergrad. Why?"

"Just wondering. I was poking around your website the other day trying to piece it all together."

"Piece what together?" I hold my breath, afraid of the answer.

I'm grateful Austin's looking at the fire, that he can't see the nervous energy that's making a nerve twitch beside my right eye.

"Whether we were in school around the same time," he says. "If you were off at college while I was off at the police academy. It's this game I play sometimes."

"Game?"

He looks up a little sheepishly and shrugs. "Like what's the closest we ever came to meeting each other before? I was in Connecticut in third grade for a Boy Scout trip. What if we crossed paths at the grocery store and never knew it?"

There's something so adorably earnest in his expression that my breath catches in my throat. "You got your degree in criminology at Portland State, right?"

"How'd you know that?"

I smile, relieved to be on safer ground. "You're not the only one who can stalk a company website."

Austin grins and flips one of the foil packets in the fire. "Touché. Yeah, I got my undergrad there. Why?"

"That's one of the universities I looked at for grad school," I tell him. "I didn't end up going there, but maybe we stood in line together waiting for coffee. It could have happened."

"No way."

His words are so definite, so certain. "How do you know?" My defenses prickle again as I contemplate Austin's super-secret spy powers.

He grins, dissolving all the icy little shards in my veins. "Because I would have talked to you," he says. "I would have seen you there with those green eyes and that knockout body, and I would have introduced myself and asked you out."

"Really." I infuse my voice with just enough skepticism to downplay the flirtatiousness of the word. And the fact that I desperately want to jump him. "What makes you so sure I'd have said yes?"

"You might not have," he admits, smiling as he nudges one of the bundles out of the fire. "But you'd have remembered me. I would have made sure of it."

The words would sound almost ominous coming from anyone else, but from Austin, they're the truth. They're charming and sweet and the absolute, one-hundred-percent truth.

God.

What if it were as simple as that? The truth, the whole truth, nothing but the truth. I open my mouth to say it. To blurt out everything, the whole ugly story.

But Austin stands up and gestures with a goofy flourish at the foil bundles. "Dinner's ready, madam. I trust you brought the appropriate fork?"

I close my mouth and swallow, nodding as I force my mouth into something resembling a smile. "But of course."

CHAPTER 11

AUSTIN

I bring a flashlight for our walk from the campsite to the hot springs, but we don't need it. The moon is plump and silver with a million stars shimmering around it like tiny disco balls.

"I can't believe this." Bree grips my hand tighter as a shooting star flickers past. "I thought the skies were clear out at the ranch, but this is insane."

"No light pollution whatsoever." I glance back at the campsite where Virginia is curled next to the extinguished embers of our campfire. The wildfire risk is minimal out here this time of year, but my dog's not taking any chances. "It helps not having city lights anywhere nearby. Not many people live close."

"Or hang out at the hot springs in the dark?" She shoots me a knowing look as she tilts her head toward the totally vacant pools. "I like how you timed this so no one else is around."

"Guilty as charged," I admit. "I wanted you to see it at night. But I also knew we'd have the place to ourselves at this hour on a Tuesday in late September."

"You don't sound too guilty to me." She grins. "Besides, I think it's a totally forgivable offense."

She's wearing a soft green sweater and a pair of sweatpants so roomy, I wonder if she borrowed them from one of her brothers. She looks utterly adorable, and I'd want to strip them both off her if I hadn't just pictured her brothers.

Fine. I want to strip her anyway.

But she takes care of it for me. Crossing her arms at the waist, she grabs the hem of the shirt and lifts it over her head. I hold my breath like a teenager watching his first skin flick, praying someone doesn't show up and change the channel. Bree's face reappears as she tugs the shirt off her bun and grins at me. "You going to strip, Officer Studmuffin, or are you going to stand there gawking all night?"

I manage to get my jaw closed, but barely. Holy shit, Bree looks amazing in a white bikini top. It's one of those stringy kinds with the little laces crisscrossing around her ribcage and back. The straps in front form a picture frame for her cleavage, and holy God in heaven, I've never seen anything as perfect as Bree Bracelyn's cleavage.

"Gawking," I reply. "If gawking all night is an option, I choose gawking."

She laughs and tosses the shirt at me. I catch it with one hand, loving the feel of her body heat trapped in the warm sweater. "I'm getting in," she says. "You're welcome to join me if you want."

She puts one hand on my arm, steadying herself as she shimmies the sweatpants over her hips and steps out of them. She drops them onto the bench beside me but doesn't let go of my arm right away.

"Which one's your favorite?"

I'm looking at her breasts, and it takes me a second to realize she's not asking an opinion on right versus left. "The big one," I manage, then clarify. "The larger pool closest to us."

She stands there bathed in starlight, pale skin glowing like she swallowed the moon. I can't stop staring at her, not even as she walks to the edge of the first pool and dips a toe into the steaming water.

"Oooh, it's perfect."

So is she, but I don't say this out loud. She already called me out for gawking, so I should probably quit doing that and join her in the water. I somehow manage to peel off my own sweat-shirt and kick my flip-flops aside before starting for the pool. I remember I'm still holding Bree's shirt, so I fold it neatly and set it on the bench beside her sweatpants.

She's already lowered herself into the rock-lined pool, and I look down at her through the water, admiring the ripple of moonbeams on her breasts. Fuck, she's beautiful. And I'm already half-hard, so I'm glad she's looking at the stars and not me.

I sink down beside her, sighing as the silky water folds around me.

She looks up and smiles. "Hey."

"Hey yourself."

Swirling her fingers through the water, she grazes my chest with her wrist. I wonder if it's intentional. If she's even half as eager to touch me as I am to touch her.

"The water feels different," she says. "Slippery or something. Like silk."

"It's silica," I tell her. "The hot springs have all kinds of minerals in them, but silica's the main one."

"I love it," she says. "It's like floating in a pool of melted butter."

I laugh and brush her knee with my hand, loving how slippery-smooth her skin feels. "I'm sure there's a fancy fork for that."

Bree grins and tilts her head back to look at the stars. She's right, they're amazing out here. I spot the big dipper and use that as a reference point to find the rest of the constellations. There's Orion and Ursa Major and—

"We should have brought one of those bottles of beer to

share." She shifts a little on the stone bench so she's leaning against me. Her hand flutters through the water again, and I nearly die when it comes to rest on my knee. "I saw some in the cooler."

"No glass allowed in the hot springs area," I say without thinking.

She turns and smirks at me. "Are you always such a rule follower?"

"Pretty much," I admit.

"I noticed you stayed the speed limit the whole way here," she teases. "Even when we were out on that long stretch of highway where there weren't any cars in sight."

"I'm a cop," I point out. "I try to minimize the amount of law breaking I do."

"Hmmm," she says, snuggling back against my chest. Her hair tickles my nose, and I breathe in the flowery scent of her hair. "I'll bet I can come up with at least one law you've broken."

I laugh and trail my fingers down her arm. She shivers, clenching her hand around my thigh. "How do you figure?"

"Have you ever sung Happy Birthday out loud to someone at a restaurant?"

"Of course," I tell her. "My other sister, Katie—her girls love doing birthday parties at this pizza place downtown when they visit. We always sing there."

"That's illegal," she says, tipping her head back to stare at the stars. "The song is copyrighted. There was this big lawsuit about it a while back where the American Society of Composers came after the Girl Scouts for singing that song and a bunch of others around the campfire."

"Are you making this up?" If she is, I don't care. I could sit here all night stroking her arm and listening to the soft lilt of her voice.

"I'm totally serious," she says. "I mean, it's not like it's enforced a whole lot, but you've totally broken the law, Sergeant Sexypants."

Sergeant Sexypants. I should probably scoff, but I dig that she has these pet names for me. And that she just shifted again so her breast brushed the side of my arm. Is she doing this on purpose, trying to make me crazy? If so, it's working.

"I Googled weird laws like you told me to a few weeks ago," she says. "Besides the whole thing about silly string being illegal in Alabama and sex shops being illegal in Georgia—"

"Sex shops are illegal in Georgia?"

"Yep." She giggles. "No vibrators for you the next time you're in Atlanta."

"I'll make a note of it," I say, secretly thrilled that Bree's the one steering the conversation into sexy territory. "So I've been breaking the law all this time," I say. "Singing Happy Birthday in public places."

"It's a shame," she says with a soft sigh. "Guess I'll have to perform a citizen's arrest."

"Want me to go get the handcuffs?"

"Not just yet," she says, and the flirty note in her voice makes me dizzy. "Do you own a Sharpie?"

"What?"

"A Sharpie. A permanent marker." She turns to look at me again, and her mouth is so close I could kiss her. I *want* to kiss her, badly. "Pretty much every state has an anti-graffiti law that makes it illegal to have any broad-tipped indelible markers in public places because they can be used to commit acts of vandalism."

Her hand moves as she's talking, sliding inch by glorious inch up my thigh. I don't know if she's aware that she's doing it, but I want her to keep going. To slide that slick little palm up the leg of my shorts and—

"I hereby pledge to get rid of all my permanent markers the second I get home." I hold up one hand like I'm swearing an oath, and it's all I can do not to slide it down through the water to cup her breast. God, I want her.

"Hmmm," she says, pretending to think. "I don't know if that's enough. You should probably face some sort of punishment."

Dear God, yes. I brush a curl back behind her ear and consider trailing my finger down her throat. "I love that you went out and Googled weird laws," I say. "Might have to make you an honorary cop."

"I accept." Her tone is flirty, and her body is warm against mine. "I'm already virtuous and saintly and committed to following all the rules." She flutters her lashes, perfectly straight-faced, but a grin tugs up the corners of her mouth. "A bastion of purity."

God, that mouth. I want to taste her again, to devour the raspberry softness of those lips. My whole body aches with the urge to have her.

Something flickers in her eyes, and for a second, I wonder if she's read my mind. She licks her lips and edges closer to me on the slippery stone bench.

"You know, it really is too bad you're such a rule-follower," she murmurs.

"Why's that?"

"Because I'm guessing there's a rule about public nudity in the hot springs," she says. "And right now, I'd really like to take off my top and have your hands all over me."

My mouth goes dry, and my dick springs to life. It's a fact Bree is well aware of, since her hand just slid the rest of the way up my thigh and is now stroking me through my swim shorts.

I lean closer, close enough to whisper in her ear. "That's where you're wrong, sweetheart." My fingers find the laces on the back of her bikini top. "This place is clothing optional after nine."

I move back in time to see her eyes widen, and I'm not sure if she's more shocked by my words, or by the feel of her bikini top slipping free as I tug the laces.

But she makes no move to stop me. "No kidding?"

"Scout's honor," I murmur. "And before you ask, yes, I really was a Boy Scout."

"Duh." The word gets muffled by her mouth colliding with mine as I claim her lips again. Our tongues tangle like we've done this a thousand times before, and Bree moans against my mouth as I finish untying her top.

Her breasts float free, and I scoop both palms beneath them. Her skin is silky and hot, and I've never felt anything so fucking good in my life.

"God, Austin." Her voice is quivery and wild as my thumbs stroke her nipples. She arches against me, moaning as I squeeze her softly. She tastes like summer fruit and desire, and the flowery smell of her hair makes me dizzy.

I pull her onto my lap like she's weightless. She floats against my chest, the apex of her thighs nesting perfectly against me. She grinds against my arousal, circling her hips like she's already got me inside her.

"Christ, you feel good," she pants.

"So do you." I seize the chance to kiss my way down her throat, licking the salty warmth of her pulse before my chin dips into the steaming water. I'm still cupping her breasts, and I lift her up in the water so I can bury my face between them. She's so damned delicious. I circle one nipple with my tongue, then the other, alternating between the two until I'm dizzy.

I can't get enough of her. I'm drowning in heat and desire and so much softness. The hungry sounds she's making in the back of her throat are enough to bring any man to his knees. I'm grateful I'm already sitting, grateful she's straddling me and rubbing against me and leaving no doubt we want the same damn thing.

"Wait." I catch her wrists as she's untying the drawstring at my waist, and she looks up at me with curiosity in her eyes.

"What's wrong?"

"Not a damn thing." I swallow hard, not wanting to kill the

mood by bringing up annoying details like sanitation in a public pool or the reliability of condoms in hot mineral water.

This stuff never comes up in my sisters' chick flicks.

Bree reads my mind, because her face breaks into a grin, and she squeezes the hardened length of me through my swim trunks. Then she slips off my lap. "Race you back to the tent."

She doesn't have to ask twice. Both of us spring out of the water and shuffle into our flip-flops, sprinting away like beach-front bank robbers. We drop several articles of clothing along the way, but neither of us stops. We're laughing as we make it to the campsite, breathless and dripping and clutching each other's hands. Virginia barks once but doesn't move from her spot by the fire pit.

My hands are slippery as I unzip the tent. We dive through the flap and bounce onto the air mattress, panting from running and from wanting each other so damn much.

"Careful there, Lieutenant Loverboy," she says when I catch the bottom of a sleeping bag in the zipper.

And there it is. The reminder she hasn't forgotten who I am, what I do. I turn to see it flicker across her face, but it's nothing like the blaze of heat in her eyes.

I reach for her again, pulling her on top of me as I lie back on the air mattress. I'm feeling smug that I had the foresight to set up our bed, to zip the damn sleeping bags together instead of fumbling out an awkward question about what sleeping arrangement she'd prefer.

If there was any question before, there isn't one now. We claw at each other's bathing suits, tugging at wet strings and damp fabric until we're blessedly, gloriously, naked together.

"Bree," I breathe against the side of her throat. "I want you so much." I glide my hands down her back and up again, memorizing the curve of her ass, the way her body fits perfectly against mine.

"Please, Austin," she begs. "Don't make me wait. Tell me you've got a condom and I don't have to find my purse."

I grin and reach over my head to the little pocket that's meant for flashlights and tissues and whatever the hell else you need handy when you're camping. Right now, it holds three condoms.

"Your wish is my command," I tell her as I pull out one of them. "Anything you want. *Anything.*"

She grins in the moonlight trickling through the tent's vented ceiling. "Thank God you're a Boy Scout. Be prepared or whatever the motto is."

I'm not feeling much like a Boy Scout as I tear open the wrapper and somehow get the condom on with Bree still straddling me. If that doesn't deserve a merit badge, I don't know what does.

She spreads her legs, letting her thighs fall on either side of my hips. Her eyes lock with mine and she smiles again.

There's no hesitation. No, *are you sure?* or any of the other questions I'd normally throw out there to make sure I've got enthusiastic consent.

Bree's consent is her sinking down hard and slick onto my cock, taking me in with one sharp thrust of her hips. "Holy Christ," she gasps, eyes wide as quarters. "You're huge."

"Do we need to slow d—"

"No!"

She starts to move, hips grinding to a rhythm that's coursing through both of us. I grab her waist, thrilled by how soft she is. How fluidly she's moving, how snug she feels around me. I pray I can hold on for more than a few seconds, but she feels so fucking good.

Gone is reserved Bree, the Bree who makes polite conversation with journalists and knows which fork to use for escargot.

This Bree is wild and primal and I fucking love her.

It.

I love *it,* not *her,* obviously. What kind of idiot falls head over heels in love with a woman he barely knows, a woman he met less than three weeks ago who's not even sure she wants to date him?

But as Bree sinks onto me again and drags her nails down my chest, the words rattle in my brain like pennies in a soda can. I can't shake them out.

"Austin!" She throws her head back and cries out, and I know in that instant it's the truth.

I'm in love with Bree Bracelyn.

The realization hits the same instant the orgasm grabs hold and yanks me over the edge with Bree. She's screaming and panting and collapsing on top of me, and it's the best fucking experience of my life.

I love you.

I stroke a hand down her back, not daring to say the words out loud. I couldn't possibly, not now, not yet.

But as she drifts to sleep on my chest, I know without a doubt it's true.

CHAPTER 12

BREE

I'm smiling like an idiot as we drive away from the empty campsite the next afternoon. I seriously couldn't wipe this grin off my face if I used sandpaper and acid.

I can't stop thinking about all three condoms and the glorious ways we used them over the last few hours. Holy shit, that was amazing.

"Don't let me forget to do that background check."

And there goes my smile. I turn to Austin, who's staring straight ahead at the road with both hands on the wheel.

"What?" I manage to keep the wobble from my voice, but just barely.

"On Meredith's boyfriend." He glances over and gives me an odd look. "I told Kim I'd check into him and make sure he's not a convicted felon or something."

"Oh. Yes. Eddie. I remember."

Austin looks back at the road, then at me again. "You okay?"

"I'm perfect." I paste the smile back on and reach over to rest my hand on his thigh. That's always an effective distraction. "Thank you for the amazing trip."

He smiles back, and I feel his thigh relax beneath my palm. "No problem. I'm glad you decided to break your no-cop rule."

"So am I."

I am, I really am, except—

I glance back at him. At those chiseled features, those blue eyes so focused on the road ahead. Last night, though, they were focused on me. There was an intensity in them I'd never seen before, something besides sex. An emotion that looked an awful lot like love, though that's silly. It's too fast, isn't it?

But hell, I'm right there with him. I don't know how it happened, but I'm crazy-stupid-head-over-heels for Austin Dugan. I love his smile and those warm blue eyes. I love his sense of honor and his Boy Scout background. I love *him,* even though I know that's the craziest thing in the world.

You can't love him. Not until he knows the whole you. Not until he knows what happened.

I glance back at him and bite my lip. Maybe I should tell him. Not the love thing, but the other. What happened thirteen years ago. I could rip off the Band-Aid fast and see what happens.

I hesitate. How the hell do you bring up something like this?

"Tell me some more dumb things you've done," I say.

He looks at me like I've just suggested we cover ourselves in tar and lie naked in the road. "Come again?"

"Like you were telling me at my place the other night," I remind him as my brain snags on the memory of Austin's fingers inside me that same night. I press on, keeping my hand on his thigh to remind myself why I'm doing this. "There was the story about lighting your hand on fire, and the one about talking to the mannequin and—"

"This is your idea of post-sex pillow talk?" His voice is teasing, but his expression is curious. "Inviting me to embarrass myself?"

"We're past the pillow talk and on our way home," I point out.

"I just wanted a reminder that you're human. That you do dumb stuff, too."

There. It's a start, a hint that there's something I want to confess. I hold my breath, waiting.

"Let's see," Austin says. "Did I tell you about the time I interviewed for an internship at this big city police department in college?"

"I don't think so."

"It went well," he says. "I was nervous as hell, but I felt good about how I answered the questions. After it was over, I got up and shook everyone's hands." He gives me a cockeyed grimace. "Then I turned and walked into the coat closet."

I bust up laughing, trying to imagine it. "Did they try to warn you?"

"That's the thing, they were busy talking and looking at each other and not me," he says. "It was a big closet, and I got all the way inside before I realized what I'd done. For a few seconds I thought about just pulling the door closed and hiding out in there for the rest of the afternoon."

"What did you finally do?"

"I walked out and gave them this sort of sheepish wave and said, 'closet's all clear. I checked it for contraband.' *Then* I left through the real door." He smiles. "I got the internship."

"That's awesome." I'm still laughing, which feels good. I love that he's so self-aware, so willing to laugh at himself. Humor is one of my favorite things about him, but it's not quite the tone I want for what I need to tell him. "Tell me another one."

"Uh, okay." He thinks about it a minute. "A few years ago when I was still a beat cop, a female officer caught me in the parking lot on my way to my car and said, 'do you have a sec?' I wasn't very busy that day and I thought I was being all witty and clever when I answered, 'I have a lot of secs.'"

"Ooof."

"Yeah." He makes a face. "The second I heard myself say that out loud, I fell all over myself apologizing. It was…awkward."

"I hope she was understanding?"

"Yeah. She laughed. She still gives me shit about it sometimes, so at least she wasn't offended."

"That's good. That it didn't turn into a sexual harassment suit or something."

I move my hand from his thigh to my own lap and wonder if there's a way to steer this to a more serious zone. I can't really segue from laughter into what I need to say.

"Tell me another one," I say. "A more serious one this time."

He looks at me oddly, keeping both hands on the wheel. "You want a grim story about me embarrassing myself?"

"Yes, please." I lace my fingers together on my lap and try not to notice my hands are shaking.

"Let's see," he says. "There's the time I went to—"

Rrrrrring!

Austin stops talking but keeps his eyes on the road. He slows the truck to a crawl and pulls into the shoulder, both hands still locked on the wheel.

"What's wrong?" I ask.

"That's the emergency ringtone I set for work," he says as the phone buzzes again. "Must be something urgent if they're calling on my day off."

Of course, Austin is one of those guys who obeys the law to the letter, waiting until the truck is completely stopped to pull his phone out of his pocket and answer the call. "Lieutenant Dugan."

I can't hear what's being said on the other end of the line, but I watch Austin's handsome face crease into a frown. "Are you sure?"

More frowning as Austin grips the wheel hard with his free hand. "If she doesn't testify, that son of a bitch could walk. I don't care how long it's been, you know what he did."

I've never heard him sound so intense. Gone is jovial, smiling

Austin. Hard-assed cop Austin has replaced him, and he's not happy.

I might find the intensity sexy if his words weren't turning my skin to gooseflesh.

"So I'll go there," Austin says. "She won't come to us, I'll go to her. I'm not letting the family go through another goddamn trial."

Beside me on the bench seat, Virginia pricks her ears and whines. I stroke a hand down her back, soothing myself as much as her.

"I don't fucking care how old Zonski was at the time," he says. "And I don't care how much time has passed. A crime is a crime, and that was a goddamn adult one. We can't just wave the wand of forgiveness and make it go away. A kid lost his life, Jim—do you seriously not remember that?"

More silence as my stomach fills with curdled lemon. I concentrate on petting the dog, on keeping my heart steady, on trying not to look guilty.

"Thank you for the update," he says. "I'll make some calls as soon as I'm back."

Then he switches off the phone.

He shoves it back in his pocket and turns to me with a sheepish look. "Sorry about that."

"Is there a problem?" My voice is a croak, and it's all I can do to force my mouth into a timid smile.

"Yeah, it's—hell, I can't really talk about it. Police stuff. Just an old case that's cropping up again. You'll maybe read something about it in the paper soon, but I can't say much until it's public."

"You're not—are you in danger? Or is the community?"

"No. God, no." He smiles and puts a hand on my knee. "Don't worry, it's got nothing to do with you or us or any of our liveli-hoods or well-being."

He's wrong about that. Not this case, that's not what I mean. I believe him when he says it's old news and nothing to start locking my doors over or carrying a shotgun to the bakery.

But the words he just said, those matter.

I don't care how much time has passed.

A crime is a crime.

We can't just wave the wand of forgiveness and make it go away.

I swallow back the lump in my throat and force myself to smile.

"I hope it all works out," I say. "Let me know if I can help."

"Thanks," he says, flashing me a tight smile as he eases the truck back out onto the road. "I appreciate that."

And that's when I know.

No matter what, I can't tell him. I can never breathe a word of my secret to Austin.

I close my eyes and accept that as the highway hums beneath our tires and the miles slip slowly behind us.

* * *

I'VE BEEN HOME LESS than a day when my brothers summon me to an emergency resort owners' meeting.

Since Ponderosa Resort is owned solely by us, it's just my brothers and me in a conference room with a big pile of Sean's famous Dungeness crab-stuffed mushroom caps and a bottle of Pinot Noir.

"I threw these together for Genevieve Dugan after she called yesterday to ask if she could bring her producer over," he says as he pours wine into each of our glasses. "She swooned."

"I can't believe you didn't call me." I scoop three mushrooms onto my plate and give Sean a stern look. "It's such a huge deal, I would have come back to help."

"Which is exactly why we didn't call you," Mark grumbles as he shovels half-a-dozen mushrooms onto his own plate. "We had it covered."

James—the only one of us who isn't dressed like he's settling onto the couch for movie night—flips his necktie over one shoulder and rolls up his sleeves. "I asked to see a boilerplate contract, just to get a feel for how they run things. It might be premature, but I'd like to get a jump on the contract terms and legal nuances of doing a show like this. The fun stuff."

Spoken like a recovering attorney, which is precisely what he is. As James leans forward to claim a spoonful of butter sauce for his own plate of mushroom caps, I survey my siblings.

"Thank you for giving her a second tour," I say. "That seems like a good sign, right? That she came back out again."

"Yep." Sean grins. "Pretty sure it's my food pushing us over the edge."

He's kidding, but he's probably right. Having a Michelin-starred chef in charge of the resort's culinary offerings has done wonders for putting us on the radar of the wealthy clientele we've been targeting. We're all good at our jobs—James, Mark, even me—but none of us has Sean's world-famous reputation.

"This calls for a celebration," I tell them.

Mark looks at me. "What the hell does it look like we're doing?"

"You called this a meeting," I point out.

"*James* called it a meeting." Sean pours a couple extra table-spoons of wine into our oldest brother's glass and shoves it in front of him. "A good indication he needs to loosen up."

"And we're talking about business stuff," I continue. "So it's a meeting."

"It's a meeting with wine and hors d'oeuvres," Sean points out. "That makes it slightly more tolerable."

James picks up a thick folder of documents and taps them on the table. "I took the liberty of printing out—"

"Bree's right," Mark says, wiping his thick lumberjack beard with a napkin. "We should celebrate. Talk about fun shit instead of work."

James frowns, possibly because his vocabulary does not

include the words "fun shit." He sighs. "What do you want to talk about?"

"Bree's romantic hot springs trip." Sean shoots a knowing look at Mark. "We've been wondering how it went."

"We don't want to hear sex stuff," Mark clarifies.

"But we do want to know how serious things are with you and the cop." Sean takes a sip of wine and leans back in his chair. "Could be handy having a police chief in the family."

James gives him a withering look. "Why, are you planning something illegal?"

Sean grins back. "I like to have options. It's nice of Bree to look out for us like this, hooking up with a cop and all."

I'm beginning to think my brothers are a pain in the ass. And also I might prefer a business meeting.

Sean sets his wineglass on the table and looks at me, a sliver of seriousness in his teasing expression. "Seriously, you're the nosiest person I know when it comes to everyone else's love life," he says. "Brandon and Jade. Amber and me. It's our turn to bug the shit out of you."

"Very mature," I mutter.

"Well it's not like we got to grow up putting lizards in your bed or yanking your pigtails," Mark points out. "All that stuff brothers are supposed to do to their sisters."

Sean nods in agreement. "We're making up for lost time."

James sighs, recognizing the fact that he's lost control of this meeting. He reaches for his wine and takes a healthy slug. "So you're dating a police officer," he says.

"The soon-to-be chief of police," Sean corrects. "Top dog. The big man."

Mark's studying me over his empty plate. "You've thrown in the towel on your no-cops rule?"

The way he's looking at me makes my forearms prickle with tiny goosebumps. He doesn't know my secret—none of them do

—but Mark's staring like he can read my mind. Does he suspect something? Or did Dad maybe tell him about—

"I'm growing as a person," I say, infusing my voice with enough maturity and confidence that I sound convincing. "It's okay to change your mind about things. To change your outlook on life and love and dating and…"

I trail off, aware that I'm talking like a self-help book. Maybe I should have insisted we stick to calling this a business meeting. I look to James for rescue. "Should we talk about this month's financials?"

"No." He picks up his wineglass and drains half of it, tugging his tie loose with his free hand. "You and I have plenty of time to go over that on our way to the Portland meeting next week."

"Fine." I turn to Sean. "Did I miss anything with the travel journalists? They're staying apart, doing their day trips, behaving like grownups instead of horny teenagers at summer camp?"

Sean snorts and takes a sip of wine. "We already went over this," he says. "We didn't manage to run this place into the ground in the twenty-four hours you were gone. It's okay to relax a little, Bree."

"We've got things covered," James says. "The staff is well-trained, and the rest of us have everything under control."

Mark nods, still watching me with that look. "You can trust us, you know. With anything."

I nod like a dumbass and look away, intent on filling my plate with more mushrooms, refilling my wineglass, adjusting my napkin, doing anything but acknowledging there are some things my family can't do for me.

Not then. Not now. Maybe not ever.

CHAPTER 13

AUSTIN

I'm at my desk Friday morning, plowing my way through a pile of paperwork, when my sister walks in. She has two Starbucks cups and an expression like the one she'd get as a kid after sneaking a handful of gingersnaps from our mom's cookie jar.

"Don't tell," Kim says, handing me one of the cups as she slips into the chair across from me. "Mom's watching Ainslie because I was supposed to have a dentist appointment, but they canceled on me at the last minute and I didn't tell mom because I desperately wanted an hour to myself and does that make me a bad mother?"

Kim's the best mom I know—outside our own, of course—so I'm pretty sure that's a rhetorical question.

"You're a great mother," I assure her. "And also a fantastic sister for bringing me coffee. How'd you know I'd need it?"

"Lucky guess," she says. "And also I saw the paper this morning. That Zonski guy's lawyers officially filed the motion for retrial."

I frown and take a sip of the coffee. It's scalding and bitter and exactly what I need right now. "Yeah. I'll have to testify again if he gets it. So will the sister, the girl who survived."

It was one of the worst cases I ever worked. An angry sixteen-year-old, blitzed out of his mind on meth and booze and whatever the hell else he'd ingested, drove his eight-year-old twin siblings home from school. Only they never made it to the house. He went off a cliff and into a tree, killing the brother instantly, and somehow managing to survive the crash himself. God bless airbags. Or not. The surviving sister remembered her brother's words before he plunged them over that cliff.

"It's time to fucking die," he'd screamed. *"You assholes are coming with me."*

Hearing that poor girl tell the story in her shaky, tear-filled voice literally brought me to my knees, and I'm mad as hell it's coming up again.

Bree must've seen the paper, too, since she called this morning to ask about it.

"That must be so gut-wrenching," she said after I filled her in on the history of the case. "I'm sorry you're having to go through this. I wish I could help."

"I'm not worried about me," I told her. "It's the family—the fact that they'll have to live through it all over again. That's not the kind of thing people just move past, you know? The death of a kid, it's the worst kind of tragedy a family can face."

"I'm sure it's hard for the police, too," she said. "For you."

"Yeah," I admitted. "I still see those three kids' faces in my dreams. Nightmares, really. It changes you, being so close to a case like that."

I've never shared that with anyone before. Bree must've heard the emotion in my voice, because I could swear I hear tears in hers, too. "Austin, I'm so sorry," she murmured. "So, so, *so* sorry."

"Thanks," I told her. "I sure lov—loved spending time with you the other night."

I almost said it. So damn close to telling her I love her, that

I've fallen head over heels for her. I held off then, but maybe I won't tonight. It's Friday, so we're getting together at my place for dinner. Bree agreed to spend the night.

"Earth to Austin!" My sister waves a hand in front of my face, bringing me back to the present. "Hellllllooo. Anyone home?"

"Very funny." I take a sip of my coffee. "Thanks again for this."

"What were you daydreaming about? You got this goofy look on your face."

"Nothing."

Kim grins, knowing damn well there's a story here. "Is it Bree?" She sips her coffee, looking positively gleeful. "Come on, indulge an old married lady. I want to hear about your girlfriend."

I don't correct her, even though I'm not positive Bree's my girlfriend. But what else do you call someone you're sleeping with and crazy about when you're pretty sure she feels the same?

"We're taking it slow," I say noncommittally. "But I'm hopeful."

Kim makes a face. "See, now why can't Meredith do that? She's been dating Icky Eddie for weeks and they're already talking about moving in together."

That jolts me out of my own little dream world. "Meredith and Eddie?" I frown. "Seriously?"

Kim groans "Yep. She thinks he's going to propose.

Crap, that reminds me. "I've been meaning to do a background check on Eddie. What's his last name?" I pivot to grab my notepad, flipping the cover to reveal a blank page.

"Dimwit," she says. "Or maybe it's Dewit."

I click my pen and scribble the name, along with a couple alternate spellings. Might as well check for aliases, too. "I'll do it at lunchtime."

"Why not now? I want to see."

"The program I use for background checks is strictly confidential," I tell her. "I'll let you know if I find anything interesting."

"Fine." She makes a face and slumps back in her chair. "Do we need to do one for Bree?"

"What?"

She shrugs and sips her coffee. "Between you and Dad, every guy who's ever looked twice at us has gone through a background check. Just wondering who's doing it for you."

"Don't be dumb." I'm dimly aware that I sound like a five-year-old version of myself when Kim would tease me about wetting the bed. "Bree's about as squeaky clean as they come."

Kim shrugs again, not looking particularly concerned. I get that she's desperate for excitement, so I'm not taking her suggestion personally. "Remember that one guy—the accountant Meredith brought home four years ago? Brent or Brett or—"

"Britt," I mutter. "Yeah. We all thought he was finally going to be Meredith's steady guy."

"He might have been, if he hadn't forgotten to mention he had a wife in Florida."

"Minor detail." I still hate the guy. "I'm pretty confident Bree doesn't have a husband. Or a wife," I add before my sister can interject.

Still, would it hurt to check?

Stop. That's silly, and besides…I trust Bree.

My sister shrugs and takes another sip of coffee. "Suit yourself," she says. "All I'm saying is that you have the resources at your fingertips. Might as well put them to use."

"I'll think about it," I say, mostly so we can end this conversation. "I'll do Bree after I do Eddie, if only so I can have the satisfaction of telling you you're an idiot."

She laughs. "Don't give me that look. I love Bree. Hell, if I didn't have a great husband and if I batted for the other team, I'd totally steal her away from you. Even if she's secretly a serial killer." My sister glances at her watch and stands up. "I should get back. Mom's expecting me at noon, and I'll probably have to come clean about the dentist appointment getting cancelled."

"I doubt she'll mind watching Ainslie again," I tell her. "Hell, book eight more dentist appointments. Mom loves spoiling her."

"That's what I'm afraid of."

I get to my feet and move around the desk to give her a hug. "Thanks again for the coffee.

"No problem. And congratulations."

"For what?"

"For Bree." She pulls back from the hug and smiles at me, and there's a strange glow of sisterly pride in her eyes. Something that suggests I'm about to get some words of wisdom. "You know I'm just kidding about the criminal thing. I think she's perfect for you. I'm so glad the two of you are seeing each other."

"Thanks." My big, dumb heart throbs in my chest. "Tell Brian hi for me. And I'll text him about elk hunting."

"Sounds good."

She waves as she sashays out the door. I watch her until she skips around the corner then move back to my desk. Settling back into my chair, I stare at my notepad where I've written the variations of Eddie's name.

Edward Dimwit. Eddie Dewit. Edward Dewit.

I cue up my computer and toggle to the page where I do background checks, but it's not Eddie's name I type.

Bree Bracelyn.

Wait, no.

Breeann Bracelyn.

A twinge of guilt pinches the center of my chest, and I almost delete the words.

But there's nothing to worry about, so I hit enter.

Then I sit back and watch the words scroll.

CHAPTER 14

BREE

It's my first time visiting Austin's house, and I'm weirdly nervous putting one foot in front of the other along the short brick walkway to his front door. His place is cute, with a huge front porch and a red metal roof that glints with fading sunlight. I trail a hand over one of the bark-stripped logs and wonder what it looks like inside.

I'm about to find out.

Before I can stop it, my brain does a quick survey of the front yard and ponders whether we'd live here or in my little cedar cottage if Austin and I got married.

Stop it.

But I can't quit smiling as I knock on the door and hear the drum of Austin's footsteps approaching. I'm grinning like a big dork as he throws open the front door.

The instant I see his face, I freeze. My smile melts like an ice cube tossed in a campfire. Something's wrong. Something's very, very wrong.

"Bree," he says. "Come in."

I swallow hard, willing myself not to panic. I hesitate there on the threshold, knowing I could still run. Just get back in my car and peel away with my heart racing and my tires spitting gravel.

Escape. Run. Hide.

But I've been doing that for years, and I'm so fucking tired.

Austin's wearing jeans and a T-shirt, and his expression is perfectly neutral. Or it would look neutral to anyone who didn't know him, who hadn't looked into his eyes as he told campfire stories or shattered into a billion breathless bits inside a tent under a starlit sky.

But I've seen that Austin, so I can see it in his eyes: *He knows.*

I'm contemplating escape when Virginia Woof trots up with her furry body wagging. "Hey, girl." My voice cracks as I stoop down to scratch behind her ears. My pulse begins to slow, and I tell myself I can do this. I can get through whatever's coming. Virginia licks the back of my hand for courage, then trots off the way she came.

When I look up, Austin's watching me.

"Come on in." His voice is warm, but there's an edge to it. "We've got an hour 'til dinner's ready, and there's something I wanted to talk about with you."

If there was any doubt in my mind, that erased it. I take a deep breath and walk through the door. I'm gripping a bottle of Pinot Noir that will pair well with the pork Austin's making, holding it by the neck like it's keeping me afloat in an icy ocean. Straightening my shoulders, I follow him into the living room. The smell of roasted meat is thick and mouthwatering, but it's not hunger making my belly roil.

"Did you have any trouble finding the place?" Austin asks over his shoulder. He's two steps ahead of me and doesn't look back. I try not to take that as an ominous sign.

"No." I scan his living room, trying to get my bearings. There's a cozy-looking brown leather sofa and loveseat, plus a red and orange-striped chair facing a giant fireplace that's fringed with smooth river rock.

I stop behind the chair and grip the back of it with my free hand. Maybe I should offer the wine, but it feels like a feeble gesture. "Austin." I swallow hard, not sure what to say. "Something's wrong."

I don't pose it as a question, because duh. He looks at me for a moment, then nods. "Have a seat."

My heart is stuck in my throat as I move around the chair. I start to settle there, but Austin catches my hand. "Beside me, Bree," he says. "If you don't mind."

I don't know if this will be harder or easier with our knees touching and warmth radiating from his bare arms, but I'm not calling the shots here. He is, and I can't tell from his face whether he's angry or hurt or…what?

The one thing I am sure of is that he knows.

He *knows.*

I set the wine on the coffee table, wishing I hadn't brought it. Wishing a lot of things that have nothing to do with dinner. I toe off my canvas flats and fold myself into the smallest space possible in a corner of the loveseat. My hands are shaking as I shove them between my knees, determined not to cry.

Austin sits down next to me, his big frame sturdy and warm. He's close enough to touch me if he wanted, but he doesn't. There's a space between us that goes beyond physical distance. I study the side of his face as he rests his hands on his knees and takes a deep breath. Maybe I should say something. Break the ice first or get this over with or—

"Bree," he says softly. "I know. I know about the accident."

Accident.

I don't know whether to feel heartbroken or relieved that he phrased it that way. How much did he piece together? There's a kindness in his eyes as he studies me, and it pierces a great big hole in my chest. It's time to come clean. About all of it.

I take another shaky breath. "Well," I say slowly, surprised my voice doesn't wobble. "I guess that answers that."

"Answers what?"

I pull my knees up to my chest and look down at them for a second, anchoring myself in the tight coil of my own body. "I always wondered if sealed records are really sealed," I say. "I guess not."

When I glance up, he's got an odd look on his face, like that's the last thing he expected me to say. "It varies from state to state," he says slowly. "Law enforcement has access to a lot of things the general public doesn't. Many states that allow expunged records have laws that it can only happen once, so courts need to be able to see if—"

"It's okay." It's not okay, but I don't need to know the details. Honestly, I'm not even that surprised.

I take a deep breath and begin.

"I had a hard time making friends when I was growing up," I said. "You probably had cliques of mean girls at your school?"

He looks at me a moment, then nods. "Bree, we don't need to rifle through your whole personal history. I just wanted to—"

"It was a hundred times worse at Trillington Academy," I say, determined to get this out there. To make sure he has the whole story, all of it, not just what's in the reports. "That's not an excuse, but I want you to have the full picture."

He nods, recognizing my need to tell the story my way. "Okay."

I can't look at him while I say this, so I stare down at my knees like I'm summoning strength from designer denim.

"I was small and skinny and had bad skin and braces, and all those things made me invisible," I continue. "I didn't have friends. Not a single one. I didn't even have a roommate, since my father paid for me to have a private suite at the academy. There was no one who even smiled at me in the halls or asked to copy my homework. Not a single person."

"That sounds…difficult." His voice is even, almost emotionless, and I'm weirdly grateful. Pity would wreck me right now, and I think he knows that.

"When I turned sixteen," I continue, "my father bought me a brand-new Mercedes. Not like I had any friends to go places with, but the fact that my birthday's in November meant I was one of the first in my class to have a license. To have my own wheels. All of a sudden, the cool girls knew who I was."

I take a shaky breath and look at Austin. He's watching me with a neutral expression, with a look he's probably perfected over countless interviews with suspects. *Just tell me everything,* the look says. *It'll all be okay if you tell the truth.*

Breathing in and out a few more times to keep myself steady, I continue. "Five of us went to a party that night," I say. "I was driving. Ashley, Claire, Marcella—they were in my grade and didn't have licenses yet. Bridget was older, one of the most popular girls in the school. It seemed like such a huge deal at the time. Smart and beautiful and adored by all the teachers. She was some kind of dancer, being scouted by Julliard for—"

I stop there because my tongue is sticking to the roof of my mouth. My hands are clammy, but my mouth is like sandpaper.

"Wait here." Austin gets up and goes to the kitchen. When he comes back, he's holding two glasses of water. He hands one to me and sets the other on a coaster on the coffee table. I take a fortifying gulp, then set the chilled glass on a coaster that's magically appeared in front of me.

With another shaky breath, I continue. "It was a big deal that Bridget wanted to go with us at all," I say. "I heard she'd been grounded for something, that she wasn't allowed to see any of her normal friends that week. It didn't matter. All that mattered is that she wanted to hang out with us. With *me*, when I'd never had any friends at all, and suddenly I've got three popular class-mates and the princess of the whole freakin' school, and we're going to this party *together*."

Austin nods. His big hands are splayed over his knees, and I wonder if I'll ever feel them on me again. Tears prick the backs of my eyelids, but I don't let them fall.

"The party was two towns over," I continue. "It was loud and crazy and not at all what I expected, but I was thrilled just to be there. By the time we headed home, it was after midnight."

"This was a Saturday?"

"Yeah," I say, not surprised he knows the day. He probably knows what color ponytail holder I wore. "Ashley and Claire and Marcella were scared about missing curfew and the dorm mother smelling beer on their breath. Bridget was playing it cool, saying she'd only had two beers and it was no big deal."

When Austin speaks, his voice is low. "It wasn't just beer," he says. "That's what the report says. Three-and-a-half grams of cocaine, plus pills and paraphernalia for—"

"Yes." I press my lips together as though that might stop the words coming out of his mouth. "That's what they found in my purse. Coke and oxycontin and a pipe and a baggie of weed. It was all in there."

His eyes flicker with surprise, like he expected me to deny it. Like he thought I'd explain away all those drugs somehow. A regular person would ask questions, but Austin doesn't. He waits for me to continue, to spill out the story the way I need to tell it.

I close my eyes, summoning the strength to get through this next part. "The cops didn't search me until hours later, but everything was still in my purse," I say slowly. "They came to my father's house with a warrant. With the news that witnesses identified my car, my license plates." I swallow hard, determined to get the words out. "With the news that a man was in a coma."

Felony hit and run.

Manslaughter.

Charged as an adult.

The words echo in my head like I'm hearing them for the first time, even though it was thirteen years ago. The police delivered them in staccato bursts while I sobbed, and my father glowered before slamming the door and calling the most expensive, powerful attorneys on the East Coast.

"The police barely got to question me at all before the lawyers swooped in," I say. "They had plenty of evidence, but not as much as they could have gotten. They didn't even drug test me. I got out of it on some stupid technicality."

This is where Austin's face hardens.

I don't blame him. How many cops have been inches away from nailing the bad guy—someone they know without a doubt is guilty—only to have him plucked off the hook by some slimy, high-rolling lawyer?

"The guy survived," Austin says. "The man in the coma. The guy you hit. He eventually pulled through."

I nod, grateful for that one small blessing. "Yes. And I spent four months in a juvenile detention center."

A reform school for rich brats.

I don't say this, but Austin knows. He's done his homework. "That must have been tough."

"It was barely a slap on the wrist." I shake my head and squeeze my knees tighter to my chest. "The victim wasn't even out of the hospital yet."

Austin's silent. He's processing, and I give him time to do that. I study his hands, part of me wishing he'd reach over and lace his fingers through mine, but I know I couldn't bear it right now. That kindness, it's something I don't deserve.

Because we haven't gotten to the worst of it.

"Bree," he says softly. "People make mistakes. Teenagers especially. They do dumb things, hurtful things." He hesitates, blue eyes searching mine. "You've learned from it, right? Become a better person."

Tears flood my eyes, and I nod because I can't find my voice. I can't find a way to tell him he's wrong, that this is so much bigger than he realizes. He's such a good man, such a kind man, and I don't fucking deserve it. This is what I've known, deep down, all along. That this thing would catch up to me.

"Oh, Austin," I whisper as a tear slips down my cheek. "That's not it. This is so much worse than you think."

There's an incredulous look in his eyes, like I must be exaggerating. I wish I were. I've never wished so hard for anything.

"Worse," he repeats, like I might have forgotten the meaning of the word. "Worse than drug use and driving under the influence and fleeing the scene after you hit and nearly kill a pedestrian?"

"Austin," I choke out. I let go of my knees and press the heels of my hands against my eyes. Tears leak out from under them as I take a few deep breaths. I need to pull it together, to force out the rest of the words.

When I drop my hands, he's watching me. Those blue, blue eyes search my face for truth. For what I've kept hidden all this time.

"I've never done drugs in my life," I whisper. "Not cocaine. Not pills. Not even marijuana, and I'm living in a state where there's a legal pot shop on every corner. And I've never driven drunk. Not once, not ever."

His brow furrows with confusion, and he stares at me like I've lost my marbles. I can almost hear them rolling on the floor, along with the last nuggets of my instinct for self-preservation.

"What are you talking about?" he says. "You admitted to the police that you drove under the influence. The drugs—"

"Weren't mine." My interruption is barely a whisper, but it stops him in his tracks. "None of it was. And I wasn't behind the wheel, either."

Austin stares at me. Just stares. "There were three separate witnesses at the scene of the hit-and-run who identified you."

"Identified my *car*," I tell him. "And they all believed me when I confessed I was the curly-haired brunette behind the wheel." I laugh, but it's a hollow, brittle sound that's halfway between a sob and outright hysteria. "Of course they believed me, because what kind of idiot confesses to crimes she didn't commit?"

Austin's gaze is steady. He looks at me for so long I think he's turned to stone. That he might not say anything at all.

Then he reaches out and puts his hand on my knee. My breath catches in my throat as one big palm closes over me. I stare down at it and will myself not to cry.

"You took the fall," he says. "For someone else's crime."

I break down then, gasping for air as fat tears roll down my face. It's his touch that does it, that unravels me completely.

I keep going, struggling to get the words out. "I wanted them to be my friends," I choke. "I thought if I took the rap, it would all work out and then we could—"

That's all I manage, but I can see Austin piecing the rest together. The way my daddy hid me away those first few hours so I'd be sober by the time police came with their breathalyzers and accusations.

But I was sober already, that's the irony.

My daddy and his lawyers made sure I got off easy, just like I knew they would. Money will buy that for you.

But it can't buy everything.

"I don't understand," Austin says slowly. "How is this worse? You didn't commit the crime, Bree. If what you're telling me is true—"

"It is true." Finally, *finally*, what I'm saying is the truth.

But not all of it. Not yet.

Austin produces a handkerchief from somewhere, and I take it gratefully, mopping at my eyes and trying to contain the torrent of fluids leaking out of my face.

Look him in the eye. My own voice whispers the command in the echo-chamber of my brain. To say these next words, I need nothing between us, no gazes skittering away in discomfort. My heart stops as his blue eyes lock with mine. My whole chest is frozen, but I force my lips to move.

"Two months after the accident, those same girls went to another party. Ashley, Claire, Marcella—Bridget was driving." I take a shaky breath. "On the way home, they hit a telephone pole. Ashley was killed instantly. Claire hung on in some kind of medically-induced coma for two weeks, and then she—she—"

"She died." Austin says the words, but I can tell he didn't know. That this wasn't in the report, because why would it be? I wasn't connected to that crime. Not on paper, anyway.

But in reality, it was all my fault.

"I was locked up then, so I didn't learn about it for months," I say. "Marcella survived, but lost both her legs. And Bridget went to prison. Grownup prison, because by that time she was old enough to be tried as an adult. She wouldn't have been two months earlier, but by then she was."

"Jesus." Austin sits back on the couch with a stunned expression.

And there it is. This badass cop, the officer of the law who's seen some of the worst crimes imaginable, is shocked. By me, by the magnitude of what I've done. Of what I set into motion.

"Obviously, the whole thing was my fault," I say.

"Bree, no." His argument sounds feeble, watered down.

I mop my eyes again, then hug my knees tight to my chest. "If I hadn't taken the fall for the first accident, Bridget would never have been behind the wheel," I say. "All those other girls—they'd have gotten busted for being drunk that first night, but they'd all be safe and whole and would have husbands and families and—"

"You can't believe that." His fingers tighten around my hands, and I realize he's still holding them. I think we'd both forgotten. "I'll admit this is a lot to process," he says, "but you can't possibly shoulder all the blame here."

"Are you serious?" A horrible, dry little laugh slips out of my mouth, and I recognize I'm on the brink of hysteria. "It's absolutely my fault. *I* was the one who offered to take everyone to that party. *I* was the one who let Bridget drive my car that

147

night, even though I knew she'd been drinking. *I* was the one who said, 'Hey, pass me all the drugs and stuff, it's cool. My rich daddy will get me off and then we can all be friends, right?'"

I'm paraphrasing a little, but that's exactly how it went down. Bree—pathetic, friendless Bree Bracelyn—is the reason those girls lost everything.

Austin shakes his hand and puts his hands on my knees again. One palm cupping each, so he can look me in the eye. So he can will me to hear what he's saying. "Other people made choices here, Bree. You can't put this all on yourself."

"I can, and I do," I tell him. "It's because of me that four girls' lives were ruined. More than that. Their families' lives, too. Hell, the pedestrian—the guy who was in the coma?"

"Who survived," he says gently, like I might have forgotten.

"The medical bills practically bankrupted his family," I say.

I don't tell him that I made sure that didn't happen. That I drained one of my trust funds and donated it anonymously to his family. None of that absolves me, none of it makes things better.

"This is why." My words are weak, like someone drained all the life out of my voice. "Why I don't date cops. Or anyone else who's good and law-abiding and—and—"

"—And likely to find out?"

I shake my head, even though there's no accusation in his eyes. *Just the facts, ma'am,* but no judgement from Austin Dugan. That almost makes it worse.

"No. I mean, yes, but that's not the main thing." My eyes flood again, and I grip the handkerchief in my fist. "Because you operate under a code of ethics. Right and wrong, good and evil, law-abiding citizens and bad guys. It's what I love about you, but it's also a world I don't belong in."

His eyes flicker at the word *love*. I'm gripping the handkerchief so hard my knuckles have turned white, and the sight of Austin's hands on my knees sends a tear slithering down my cheek. "I don't deserve that, Austin," I whisper. "I don't deserve someone good and honest and *perfect*."

He snorts and rakes a hand through his hair. "Jesus, Bree. I've spent the last month proving to you how imperfect I am. The stories about lighting my hand on fire and talking to a mannequin weren't enough to convince you I'm far from fucking perfect?"

"But that's just it." I shake my head and swipe at my eyes again. "You've been honest with all the imperfect parts of you, and I've been a cowardly, lying piece of shit." I drop my knees and plant my feet on the floor, locating my shoes with the tips of my toes. I wobble as I stand, but I don't let that stop me.

"Bree, wait—"

"No." I scuff my feet into my shoes as I start for the door. "It took you less than a month to dig up all this dirt on me. How long do you think it'll take the media? To start pointing fingers at the guy who's in line to be chief."

"Bree—"

"And you're about to get pulled into a big, public trial and you know something like this could come up." I'm already halfway to the door. "Think about it; Lieutenant Dugan is dating a criminal," I sputter. "Clearly his judgement can't be trusted. You can't tell me that wouldn't happen."

Austin catches me by the arm and turns me around to face him. "Stop," he says, but I can see in his eyes that he knows my points are valid. "Just sit down and let's talk about—"

"I can't." I wrench my arm free, hating the loss of his touch. Hating myself even more. "I knew better than to date a cop. Just let this die before I end up wrecking more people's lives. *Please*."

He reaches for me again, but I'm too quick this time. I'm almost to the door now, fumbling my keys out of my pocket as I run. He could catch me if he wanted. He's bigger and stronger and faster, and he could have me pinned against the wall before I closed my fist around the doorknob.

But that's not the sort of man he is. He's gentle and kind and respectful of my space.

And he's everything I don't deserve.

Choking back a sob, I fling open the door and sprint for my car, Austin's voice ringing behind me.

CHAPTER 15

AUSTIN

*I*t's been three days, and Bree's still not answering my calls.

On day four, I drive out to the resort. The morning air is crisp and spiced with the scent of leaves and frost-crisped grass. It won't be long before we get our first snow.

Snow makes me think of bonfires and hot tubs, which makes me think of Summer Lake Hot Springs, which makes me think of Bree, though pretty much everything does these days. How the hell could she think I'd judge her for what happened thirteen years ago? Or blame her for something that wasn't her fault.

It's not about you, dumbass. It's got nothing to do with what you think.

It's my sister's voice I'm hearing in my head, though I haven't breathed a word of Bree's secret to her or anyone. She's right, my subconscious-sister-voice. Bree's not crippled by my opinion of her.

She's crippled by her own.

I'm considering this as I pull up in front of her cabin early Tuesday morning. It takes me a few seconds to spot Mark standing off to the side. He's gripping an axe and staring at a small wooden shed I never noticed before. His head snaps up when I open the car door, and he watches me without expression as I make my way up the path to the house.

"She's not here." He doesn't move a muscle, not even to set down the axe.

I give him my best cop stare and avoid looking at the heavy piece of weaponry in his hands. "You sure about that?"

He laughs, which startles me. I've never seen him do anything but glower. "Yeah," he says, wiping a faded red bandana over his forehead. "I like how you think, though. Fuck yes, I'd lie to the cops or the pope or anyone else to protect my sister. But I'm serious, she's gone."

I've gotta admire the guy's straightforwardness. And his love for Bree, which makes two of us. I lean against the side of her cabin and glance at the mountain of firewood he's stacked in the shed. Bree's set for winter. "Where'd she go?"

I don't expect him to answer. He stares at me a long time before he does. "Some financial meeting in Portland." His expression softens almost imperceptibly. "James is with her."

I haven't met the whole family yet, and I must look unsure because he adds almost kindly, "The lawyer brother. She's in good hands."

Lawyer. I roll the word around in my head, wondering whether to read anything into it. How much does Mark know? Or James or Sean or—hell, I can't remember all their names.

But I appreciate what Mark's telling me: *She's safe. She's not alone. We've got this.*

I can respect that.

"Will you tell her I stopped by?"

Mark grunts and gives a faint head-tilt that might be a nod. Not the world's most scintillating conversationalist, this brother.

I turn to go. I'm halfway to my car when I hear his voice over my shoulder.

"Don't you goddamn quit on her."

I turn back around, sure I've heard wrong. "What?"

He watches me for a second like this is a test. Like he's waiting to see what I'll do.

I stand my ground, keys gripped in one fist. I'm not going anywhere.

"Bree." He shoves the bandana in his pocket and stares at me. "She seems tough. She fucking bosses us around like it's her job, which it pretty much is, and she's good at it. She thinks she knows what's best for everyone else, and the thing is, she *does*. But she's shitty at knowing what's good for her."

He scrubs a hand over his beard, and I get the sense this is the longest string of words he's put together all week. Maybe all year. "She's headstrong and protective and bossy as hell, but she's also smart and generous and the kindest fucking person I know."

My throat pinches tight. "I know," I manage. "I know all that. Especially the kindness."

He nods once. "So don't fucking quit on her," he says. "Even if she says that's what she wants."

I grip my car keys harder, determined not to let my voice shake. Not to let Bree's brother see how much his words have rattled me. "Thank you." I loosen my grip on the keys and wonder if I should say anything else.

I'm still thinking about it when Mark shoulders the axe, then turns and stomps around the corner of the cabin. I stare at the space where he vanished, at the neatly-stacked piles of firewood.

I don't know if Mark's lying about Bree leaving town, but if it's true, she's not the only one. I've got two hours to get to the airport. I turn and make my way back to the car as a faint flicker of hope sparks in my chest.

* * *

IT'S EARLY the next morning by the time my red-eye flight

deposits me in Boston. My first interview with the potential witness in the Zonski case isn't until tomorrow, but there's a reason I flew in early. It's the same reason I paid out-of-pocket for the extra hotel night and for the rental car that carries me across state lines and into Rhode Island. Traffic is heavy, but Google driving directions get me right to the front gate of the women's penitentiary in less than two hours.

Visiting hours have just started when I walk through the door. I'm wearing jeans and a button-down instead of my uniform, but I flash my badge at the guards. I pocket it fast, determined to play this like a regular guy. Just a friend checking on something for a friend.

As soon as I'm seated, Bridget Mueller takes one look at me and frowns. "Cop."

"Yep." I fold my hands on the table. Big shocker that she's bristly about law enforcement. The trouble she got into at seventeen wasn't the beginning, and it wasn't the end, either.

She stares at me with deep suspicion, folding her tattooed arms on the table in front of her. Her short curls are bleached the color of faded straw, and she's got a scar on her right cheek. She was pretty once; I can see that. She's pretty still in an edgy, angry way.

"Who the hell are you?" she demands.

I don't beat around the bush. "A friend of a friend," I tell her. "You remember Breeann Bracelyn."

Her brows arch in surprise, but she's trying to hide it. "Yeah. Skinny little rich bitch. So?"

I keep my expression neutral, not letting her see that the attitude pisses me off. That won't get us anywhere. "You haven't forgotten the person who took the rap for you."

There's that flicker of surprise again. I expect her to deny it, but she shrugs and lifts her chin. "Statute of limitations is up. Besides, that was a long time ago."

Neither of these things is precisely true, but that doesn't matter right now. I lean back in my chair, adopting my best casual cop pose. "Tell me about what happened before the accident," I say. "When you were sixteen, before you even knew Bree."

Her eyes widen again, and I can tell I've shocked her for real this time. She doesn't even try to hide it. She knows damn well what I'm talking about, and I can see her puzzling it out. Looking for ways this could be a trap. She owes me nothing, and it's possible she'll stand up and walk away.

But she stays sitting. I watch as her expression shifts from surprise to curiosity. "Why should I tell you anything?"

"Maybe because you're ready to."

She snorts and looks down at her hands. Her nails are bitten to the quick, and there's something vulnerable in her eyes. Something I recognize from Bree's face on my couch the other night. From every suspect who's ever reached a breaking point.

When she looks up, some of that false bravado is back. "Those records are sealed." She narrows her eyes. "Why the fuck are you here?"

"Confirming a theory," I say. "For a friend."

"*Friend.*" Bridget scoffs, like it's a curse word, and I'm reminded of the tremble in Bree's voice.

"I didn't have friends. Not a single one."

I press a little harder, right where I know it'll matter. "Bree Bracelyn wasn't the only girl whose daddy knew how to bail her out of trouble," I say. "Two DUIs when you were sixteen, Bridget. And they both magically vanished the year before that accident. Before Bree took the rap for you."

She looks away, muttering something under her breath that I don't quite catch. "They couldn't prove shit," she says. "Breathalyzer was faulty. And anyway, that dumbass cop forgot to read me my Miranda rights before—"

"I don't give a shit, Bridget."

She whips her head back to look at me. "What *do* you give a shit about, huh?"

"Bree." I don't hesitate at all. "I care about Bree. About helping her get closure."

That gets me another snort. "Closure? Closure for *what*?"

"For ruining your life," I say.

I thought I'd learned all her expressions of stunned surprise, but this is a new one. She jumps like I've poked her in the ribs, mouth falling open. It takes her a few seconds to recover, and when she does, she rolls her eyes hard enough to knock them out of the socket. "Are you fucking kidding me right now?"

"Do I look like I'm kidding?"

She tries to hold eye contact, but I wait her out. After a few more breaths, she looks down at her hands again. "What do you want me to say?" She rubs her thumb over a scratch on the edge of the battered table, and I watch the web of lines deepen between her brows. "You want to hear that my daddy was a sick son-of-a-bitch who wanted everyone to think we had this perfect life in our perfect fucking mansion on the hill, but behind closed doors, he beat the shit out of my mother every chance he got. Is that what you want to hear?"

It's not at all what I want to hear, but it's the truth. It's what I pieced together from Bridget Mueller's file, so I'm not surprised.

But in a fucked-up way, I'm relieved. This isn't the first time Bridget has told someone this part of her story, but it's a puzzle piece Bree has never had.

And that's why I came here today.

"You were dealt a shitty hand from the start, Bridget." I keep my tone gentle, the one Bree called *Officer Velvet Voice*. The thought of Bree makes my chest pinch, but I keep going. "Between your dad's issues and your mom's depression and your trouble with the law starting when you were twelve—yeah, I know about the shoplifting—you got on a lousy path pretty early in life. Bree Bracelyn didn't put you there."

She looks up sharply. "Who the fuck said she did?"

I don't answer that, waiting for her to fill in the blanks. It's better that way sometimes, letting someone get there on their own.

"Bree does." She shakes her head as the reality sinks in. "Little-Miss-Goody-Two-Shoes thinks she ruined my fucking life."

"Not just yours," I say. "The other girls in the car that night."

She snorts again and looks back down at the table. "That bitch wasn't the one behind the wheel." She shakes her head like she can't believe we're having this conversation. "Claire and Ashley and Marcella were just as fucked up as I was. Not that anyone deserved to die—"

"Of course not."

"Shit." Bridget looks away, and I swear I see liquid pooling in the corner of her eye. "Bree really thinks it's her fault?"

"Yeah. She does. And it's been eating her alive for thirteen years."

Bridget grunts and returns her gaze to mine. There's defiance in her eyes, but there's something else. Something that tells me I may not have wasted a trip here.

"I know a few things about regret." She shakes her head again, and I pretend not to notice the tear that slips down her cheek. "Stupid bitch."

I've never heard those two words spoken with such an odd mix of affection and sadness. And regret. A lot of regret.

Her gaze narrows on mine. "Why the hell did she do that, anyway? Take the rap for—" She stops short, pressing her lips together.

"This isn't a trap, Bridget."

"No?" She swipes at her face with the sleeve of the long-sleeved tee she wears under her prison blues. "So what the hell is it?"

"A chance to make things right."

Her laugh comes out more like a choked sob. "Oh, that's rich."

She laughs again, but there's a flicker in her eyes. Something that looks a tiny bit like hope. When she looks at me again, her bottom lip quivers.

"How?" She sniffs. "How do I make things right?"

CHAPTER 16

BREE

"*I*'m so glad I caught you!"

I look up from my desk to see travel blogger Shawna Anders hustling into my office. She's half of the couple that runs the Wandering Hearts blog, and from the way she's beaming, I'm guessing things are going well with her other half.

The half who has—to the best of my knowledge—managed to keep his hands off Gigi from the other travel blogging duo since I embarked on my mission to keep them apart.

"Hey, Shawna." I click "save" on the marketing plan I was working on and pivot my desk chair to face her. "I saw you and Chris got checked out this morning?"

She settles herself in my guest chair with her curtain of silky blond hair falling over her shoulder the way it does in half her Instagram photos. I might hate her for being beautiful if she wasn't pretty damn nice. "I just settled up in the restaurant with your brother."

I frown and reach for a pen, though there's nothing I need to write. "All your meals were comped."

"I know, but I always like to tip extra," she says. "The service was really excellent."

"I'm glad to hear it." My fondness for Shawna cranks up a notch. I'm a big fan of anyone who remembers to take care of our waitstaff and housekeepers, even though we pay them a generous wage.

"Thank *you*," she says. "Not just for the great stay. For everything you did. *Everything*."

Her flawless features settle into a knowing look, and I wonder how much she's figured out. If she's aware of my efforts to help her idiot boyfriend keep it in his pants.

"We've got a media library of images from around the resort, so let me know if you need access," I say, sticking with my normal, professional spiel. "I'm looking forward to reading your coverage about Ponderosa."

She laughs and waves a hand. "That wasn't what I meant. I mean, coverage will be amazing. I've got Twitter posts ready to roll, Facebook, Instagram, blogs, yadda yadda yadda."

"We appreciate that," I say carefully, wondering if I can ask one of my brothers to review them this time. I'm not sure I have it in me to spend an afternoon leafing through love-infused photos and paragraphs about romantic dinners under the stars. "I'll let the rep at Travel Oregon know how great you've been to work with."

She tosses her hair and leans forward just a little. "Thanks. That's not why I wanted to come talk with you, though. I know what you did."

My heart stops. The blood drains from my face, and I wonder how she found out about the accident. "I—um—"

"Sending Chris and me on little day trips while you sent that other couple—the ones from Lovebird Journeys?"

"Gigi and Graham." Oh, thank God. *That's* what we're talking about? I shift gears and prepare to apologize for meddling in someone else's love life. "It seemed like a good idea to give you your own separate adventures to write about."

"And to keep Chris from checking out Gigi's ass by the pool?"

She laughs and waves a dismissive hand. "Of course I noticed. And I'm grateful you made sure I got all that alone-time with Chris. Because that's what it took for me to realize he's a self-centered prick. We broke up this morning."

"What?" I stare at her, not positive I've heard right. "Come again?"

She just laughs. "I suspected he was an asshole for a while, but you helped me figure it out for sure. I'm better off without him, trust me. He's already on his way back to Melbourne."

I stare at her. "Shawna. I don't know what to say."

"Congratulations would be a start." She reaches across the desk and squeezes my hand. "You look like you're freaking out, and you shouldn't be. I'm happy about this, I am."

"Okay." I swallow hard, not sure what to make of this. "The blog—"

"Was mine to start with," she says. "I own the domain, the content, the Twitter and Instagram handles—I registered all of it before I even met him. He can start his own if he wants."

This isn't the outcome I hoped for when I found out about Chris and Gigi flirting, but Shawna seems so happy that I force a smile. "Congratulations," I offer. "I'm glad for you."

"Thanks." She bounces out of her chair, long hair flying like she's posing in front of a fan. "Gotta run. I'm catching a plane to the Bahamas."

I grab my phone off the desk, still reeling from her news. "You said you just saw my brother in the bar?"

"He's polishing the glassware or something."

"I'm texting him right now." I key in a few quick words to Sean. "Go pick out any bottle of champagne you want, on the house."

"Whoa! Thanks!"

I stand up to see her out the door, and Shawna pulls me in for a hug that smells like sunscreen and the expensive herbal shampoo we stock in all the guest cabins. Usually I stick with handshakes for professional FAM tours like this, but the hug feels right, and I'm grateful for it.

"Seriously, Bree—thank you for everything."

"Don't mention it," I say. "Happy travels."

"Thanks." She pulls back and beams, then turns and flounces out the door. Her flounce halts right in the doorway as she collides with Donovan of the Nomadic Dudes travel site.

"Hey, you." They slap palms in a friendly high-five, and I remember they've done dozens of the same media trips. "Loved your piece on the top five unique spots to grab a beer in town. Sam and I are going to check out that barber shop today."

"Yes, do it!" she says. "Get the Pinedrops if they still have that on tap."

"Will do."

Shawna high-fives Donovan's husband, Sam, then jogs off toward the restaurant and her free bottle of champagne.

"Cute girl," Donovan says, stepping into my office as Sam leans against the doorframe behind him. "If you're into that kind of thing."

Sam rolls his eyes. "How about not referring to women as 'things,'" he suggests. "Or 'girls.'"

"You're forgiven," I assure Donovan as I pull him in for a tight hug. God, it's good to have friends. "Are you still having a good trip?"

"The best." He draws back and waves Sam inside. "Come on, I want to get a photo."

"Of what, my office?"

"Of us, silly." Donovan slides an arm around me and strikes a pose. "I want something to show our fellow Boilermakers how you're doing."

"This isn't going on the blog, right?" I lean into him, surprised by how grateful I feel for the human contact. I might have sucked at the friend thing when I was sixteen, but I'm glad I figured it out in college. Glad this friendship with Donovan has survived the years.

"Cross my heart, it's just for us," he assures me as Sam clicks the shutter. "And Sam's a whiz with Photoshop. He'll wipe out those bags under your eyes in no time."

"Hey—" I try to protest, but there's no point. He's right, I've been sleeping like crap lately.

"It's all right, sugar." Donovan plants a kiss on my temple and releases me as Sam flips through the images on his camera. "Man trouble will do that to you."

I can tell he's fishing, since I haven't said a word about breaking things off with Austin.

Austin.

My heart twists, and I wonder what he's doing. Mark said he stopped by a few days ago, but I haven't heard from him since. No phone calls, no text messages. I guess he finally got the message and backed off.

It shouldn't bother me. I'm the one who ended things. I'm the one who believes it could never work. It couldn't, right?

"I almost forgot!" Donovan claps his hands together and Sam and I jump. "You'll never guess who sent us a present."

"Who?"

Sam lets go of his camera and smiles. "Our favorite homophobic cowboy, Bob Mosley."

"No kidding?"

"He apologized for the incident at the café," Donovan says. "Sent us a very nice note and a bottle of rye from Oregon Spirit Distillery."

"The note was my favorite," Sam adds. "It said, 'sorry I was a redneck asshole.' Isn't that sweet?"

"That's unbelievably sweet." I swallow back an unexpected wave of emotion and channel some secret thanks to Austin. And no, he's not the one who sent the rye. I wouldn't have believed it myself if I hadn't been the one to answer the call from Bob yesterday.

"I hadn't thought about it that way before," he muttered over the phone, and I could practically hear him scuffing his boot through the dirt. "Austin's a damn smart guy. He'll make a good chief."

"That he will," I agreed weakly, wishing those words didn't sock me in the gut.

I know I made the right choice. Even though the court ruled against a retrial in the Zonski case—it was front page news this morning—there are still dozens of reasons Austin and I can't be together. In what world can a police chief make a life with an ex-con? No world I've ever lived in, that's for sure. Did I really think there was even a slimmest chance that could work?

"So we're taking off now." Donovan waves a hand in front of my face like he knows I was a million miles away. The sympathy in his eyes tells me he has a good idea who I journeyed there with. "Congrats on the resort, Bree. It's amazing."

"Thanks." I give him one more fierce hug, closing my eyes as he pulls me close. "Thank you for coming out to see the place."

"My pleasure. We'll write lots of nice things." He draws back and plants a kiss on my forehead. "I love you."

"I love you, too."

I move to hug Sam, and that's when I see him.

Austin, standing just over Sam's shoulder, a look of surprise on his face.

He recovers fast, slipping the cop mask back into place. "Bree." He straightens up, hands behind his back like he's at parade rest. "I can come back another time."

"Oooh, you must be the cop." Donovan eyes him up and down. "It's good to finally meet you."

Sam grabs his husband's hand and shoots me an "I've got this" look.

"We were just leaving," Sam assures us. "My husband and I have a cave tour to get to. Thanks for everything, Bree."

"Have fun, guys." I wave at them both until they're out of sight, then turn back to Austin with my heart thundering in my ears.

He's here. He's actually here.

And he looks ridiculously hot in his cop uniform. I can't believe I never appreciated the aesthetic in my years of not dating cops. Broad shoulders, medals and ribbons gleaming on his chest. He's off-limits, obviously, but I can still admire. It's no wonder Children's Welfare Society ladies have been hounding him to do that cop calendar.

"Your other journalists got all checked out."

"Yeah," I answer, wondering how he knows. "It's just Donovan and Sam now. I've got a couple writers coming in next week from—"

"But you're free now." He steps closer, and I can smell the piney scent of his soap. I wish I didn't still want him. "You're free for the next twenty-four hours, if I'm not mistaken?"

I blink away the haze of lust. How the hell does he know this? I open my mouth to ask, but he catches my hand in his and stops my tongue in its tracks.

"Bree, I need you," he says as my heart lurches into my throat. "For the next twenty-four hours, I need you to come with me."

I'm confused by the bigness of his hand around mine and the dizzying heat pulsing up my arm. "Come with you *where?*"

"Your brother already threw a few things in a bag for you." He's so matter-of-fact, like we've been planning a getaway for months. "You and I are taking a little road trip. You can come willingly, or I can throw you over my shoulder and carry you to the car. Which would you prefer?"

"You can't be serious."

"Dead serious."

The steel in those blue-gray eyes tells me he is. My stupid, traitorous libido leaps at the idea of being slung over Austin's shoulder like the heroine in some bizarre caveman romance flick. I shouldn't like this. He's being bossy and presumptuous, and any woman in her right mind would probably slap him.

But I'm not in my right mind, and I haven't been since I walked out of Austin's house last week. And the truth is that this whole domineering cop thing has my girl parts clenching with want.

"Austin." I use my most professional PR voice, determined to be responsible. To do the right thing instead of following my base urges. "Even if we had anything new to say—"

"I'm counting to three before I carry you."

Good Lord, he's serious.

But so am I. About a lot of things, not the least of which is that I can't tether myself to a guy who's so goddamn *good*. For crying out loud, this morning's article had a sidebar about a new community service project he's heading up with local schools. How can I drag a guy like that down to my level? I'm not that selfish. Not even if I want to be.

"Austin, I don't think—"

"One."

"We're too different, you and me. If you'd just—"

"Two." He takes a step forward.

I fold my arms over my chest and try to ignore the thudding of my heart, the clamminess in my palms. "We can't possibly—"

"Three."

He doesn't wait for a response. Just grabs me around the waist and hoists me over his shoulder like a sack of laundry.

Holy shit, he really did it.

"Your bag is already in the car." His tone is all business as he carries me across the lobby, where, thank God, there are no guests or journalists milling around. He pushes through the door, and I twist my body to look behind us. Sean's standing next to the bar, and he waves like it's the most normal thing in the world to see his sister forcibly carried to a cop car.

"Have fun," Sean shouts as the door swishes shut behind us.

"You're a dick," I growl, not sure if I'm talking to Sean or Austin. Or Mark, who probably packed the damn bag Austin mentioned. "I'm going to kill you."

"Threatening an officer," Austin says cheerfully as he strides across the parking lot. "That's a crime, you know."

"You are such a jerk."

"You want me to put you down?"

I should say yes. I know he'd do it in a heartbeat if I did. But oh my God, it feels so good to have his arms around my waist, to have my palms pressed against the muscled plane of his back. Is it wrong to like this so much?

"Where are we going?"

"Over the mountains," he says, unlocking the door of his cop car to sling me into the front seat. I guess I'm grateful it's not the back, the part with the iron bars and doors that don't unlock from the inside. "We're going to Portland."

"I just came back from Portland."

He tucks my limbs inside and pulls up the seatbelt for me before shutting the door and jogging around to the driver's side. For a guy who just orchestrated a kidnapping, he seems downright jolly.

"It's only three hours," he says as he jams his keys into the ignition. "Buckle up."

He waits for me to comply before easing out of the driveway, signaling like the upstanding citizen he is. I look around the cop car, not surprised it's immaculate. "You're kidnapping me using taxpayer resources?"

"I'm going to a statewide police conference." He adjusts something on the dash, then turns the air conditioning so it cools my heated face. "We're having a special guest speaker this year."

"You're taking me to a police conference?" Okay, that's not

what I was expecting. I don't know what I thought was happening here, what with this being my first kidnapping and all. "Why a police conference?"

"You'll see." He glances at me, his expression softening just a little. "Tell me you don't want this, and I'll turn back around now. Say 'fish fork' as your safe word or something. I might be a bossy prick, but I'm not a total asshole."

I bite my lip and glance out the window. "I know."

I do know, and it hurts my heart to realize he's such a great guy. I have no idea what he's up to, but I'd be lying if I said I wasn't intrigued. I settle back in the seat, adjusting the strap between my breasts. There's a quick spark in his eyes, and I wonder if he's remembering the way he trailed a line of kisses through that channel, dotting my skin with flecks of chocolate left over from our s'mores. My face heats up, and I reach over to crank the air conditioning.

"What are you thinking?"

It's Officer Velvet Voice. I cross my legs, hating the fact that it turns me on.

"I don't know." That's true enough. But it's time for total honesty.

"I'm afraid," I whisper. Austin taps the brakes, and I shake my head. "Not about this."

He accelerates again. "What are you afraid of?"

I consider that for a second. "When I walked into your house and realized you knew about what happened, do you know what went through my mind?"

His eyes stay on the road, but frown lines etch his brow. "I'm sorry," he says. "I could have handled that better."

"You were fine. You could have handled it like a professional shrink and I still would have had the same thought."

"Which was?"

"It's over now." My breath catches in my throat when I say it, and I realize how much I don't want that to be true. "I thought, 'oh, sure, he'll be a nice guy and say he still likes me. But deep down, he'll always wonder. About what kind of person I am or whether he knew me at all.'"

"I know you, Bree." He reaches over and rests his hand on my knee, eyes shifting to me for a few seconds before he looks back at the road. "And I'm not going anywhere."

"Except to Portland."

He smiles. "With you."

"With me." I study the side of his face. "You know this can't work, right?"

"I wouldn't have kidnapped you if I believed that."

That is either the sweetest or weirdest thing anyone's ever said to me. How is he not giving up? My throat tightens as I remember my mom's response the night my father called to tell her about the accident. About the fact that I'd be going to juvey.

"She's a lost cause now," she muttered, unaware I was listening on the downstairs extension. *"I always knew she'd disappoint us like this."*

Austin doesn't look disappointed. He looks like a man on a mission, and apparently that mission includes me. I should fight this. I know I should, for his own good.

But it feels so good here with Austin by my side, steady and stable and everything I used to wish for. Is it wrong to savor that just for a while?

"Open the glovebox," he says.

I swallow back the lump in my throat. "What?"

"The glovebox. There's something in there for you."

Perplexed, I do what he says. I pop the latch and pull out an envelope with my name on it. The handwriting is loopy and feminine, and I don't recognize it at all.

"You can read it out loud if you want," he says. "But you don't have to. I know what it says."

I shoot him a questioning look, but he keeps his eyes on the road. His expression reveals nothing. My hands are shaking as I tear open the envelope and a single piece of lined paper falls into my lap. I pick it up and unfold it slowly.

BREE,
　You dumb bitch.

I JERK my gaze to Austin. "What is this?"

His eyes stay glued to the road. "Keep reading."

I look back at the paper. What the hell is happening here?

BREE,
　You dumb bitch.
　Your cop buddy says you've spent thirteen years blaming yourself for what happened back in school, which is just fucking stupid. I screwed up. Not you. You're guilty of being too fucking nice, and that's about it. Get on with your life.
　Sincerely,
　Bridget Mueller
　P.S. Seriously, you're an idiot.

TEARS WELL IN MY EYES, and the words blur together. It's the first time in my life I've felt grateful for being name-called. I don't know what to say.

"Is this real?"

He gives me an odd look. "Of course, it's real."

"How did you get this?"

"I paid her a visit in prison," he says. "And before you start kicking yourself for playing some imaginary role in landing her there, she also gave me permission to share her rap sheet with you."

I bite my lip, not sure what to make of this. "Will it make me feel better or worse?"

"You think I'd offer if it'd make you feel worse?"

"No. But I don't want you to sugarcoat anything. Just the truth, okay?"

He gives me a look, and I recognize the irony of what I just said.

"I'm sorry, Austin," I tell him. "I'm so sorry I wasn't up-front about what I did. About who I was."

"I know damn well who you are, Bree," he says. "You're a smart, compassionate, driven woman who made some bad choices as a kid, but those don't define you."

"I also made bad choices as an adult." I crease the letter in my lap and trace the edge of the paper with the pad of my thumb. "That's what I mean, though. How can you ever trust me after this?"

"Do you have more skeletons in your closet?" he asks. "A secret career as a high-dollar escort or a history of beating puppies?"

"No."

"Okay then," he says, merging onto the highway. "You're starting from a clean slate."

I fiddle with the seatbelt. "Okay," I say softly. "Tell me about Bridget's rap sheet."

So he does.

And somewhere between stories of her pre-teen shoplifting and her first DUI and her adult career in forgery, I find an odd sort of peace. It's dumb, since I shouldn't take comfort in someone else's suffering. It must make me a shitty person, to feel better about myself because someone else screwed up.

But what it means is that I'm not the only one. Mistakes were made, but they weren't all mine. As Austin speaks, the tiniest weight lifts from my shoulders. I roll them in their sockets, listening to the smoothness of Officer Velvet Voice, admiring the

171

dedication it required for him to bring me these nuggets of information. Of redemption.

"Thank you," I murmur when he's done speaking. My eyelids feel heavy, like I've gone weeks without sleeping. Years.

"You're welcome." He reaches over and rests a hand on my knee. "You're a good person, Bree. One of the best I know."

Tears sting the edges of my lashes, and I give in to the urge to close my eyes. As the highway hums beneath us and Austin's fingers twine through mine, I almost believe him.

* * *

"Bree. Wake up, Bree."

I blink my eyes open to find Austin touching my shoulder. He's standing in the open passenger door, and it takes me a second to remember I'm in a cop car and not naked in a tent.

Sunlight funnels through a blob of rainclouds over his shoulder, giving him a golden halo effect. He looks like a freakin' hottie cop poster.

I rub my eyes with the backs of my hands. "I fell asleep?"

Duh, Bree.

Austin just smiles and holds out his hand. "Come on," he says. "The guest speaker doesn't do her thing until tomorrow, but you've got a private meeting with her in ten minutes."

My sleep-fogged brain tries to figure out why I'd get a special meeting with the guest speaker at a statewide cop conference and comes up empty. But I trust Austin enough to let him unbuckle my seatbelt and help me out of the car. My legs are shaky as I clamber to my feet, and he holds me by the elbows while I get my bearings.

I tip my head back, only meaning to look at him. Only meaning to smile, to plant one single, chaste kiss along his jawline.

That's not how it happens.

The second my lips touch his, something melts inside me. All my resistance, all my reasons for holding back, they dissolve the instant his tongue grazes mine. I clutch the back of his head and kiss him hard, needing him to know I'm through resisting. Whatever this is between us, I'm done fighting it. He's shown me he's willing to hang on no matter what, no matter how shitty I am.

I can damn well do the same.

We're both breathless when I pull back. His eyes blaze with blue heat, with satisfaction. He smiles and drops his hands from my waist. "To be continued." He grabs my hand. "Come on. Let's get inside."

Twining our fingers together, he leads me across the pavement and through the doors of a convention center I visited last year for a hotelier's conference. The air smells like rain, but pinpricks of sun spear through fine slits in the clouds. There's blue sky peeking over the horizon beyond the hotel parking lot, and bright orange maples fringe the freeway beyond that.

He pulls open the door and leads me down a corridor, past signs that point to conference rooms and the hotel coffee shop. "We've got a room upstairs, but you're meeting her first," he says.

Her?

"Austin, who are we—"

And that's when I see it. Next to a reader board advertising the locations of workshops on cybercrime and terrorism response. A life-sized poster of a woman with straight brown hair and eyes so dark they're almost navy. It's the eyes I remember, and I freeze in my tracks and stare at the face I knew so long ago.

Marcella Burkhardt.

The girl who lost her legs, who nearly died in that crash that happened while I was locked up at juvey. I stare at the image, absorbing the defiant smile, the muscular arms, the crisp, blue police uniform.

And the prosthetic limbs visible beneath the hiked-up hem of her cop slacks. I blink hard, trying to make sense of it.

Austin squeezes my hand and I turn to look at him. "She became a cop," he says. "Kind of a famous one."

My mouth is dry. I have so many questions, and I don't know which one to ask first. "How did you—"

"I recognized the name when you said it," he says. "I mean, I know there's more than one Marcella in the world, but it's not the most common name, and it was plastered all over the workshop materials for this year's conference. So I did some checking."

I look back at the poster as the puzzle pieces arrange themselves in my mind. *America's first double-amputee, active-duty police officer* read the words printed above her head. There's a spark in her eye that I know wasn't put there by Photoshop.

"She's okay," I breathe. "She's actually okay."

"Better than okay," he says. "She's kind of a legend for her motivational speeches. When she's not busting bad guys, she travels the country sharing her life story."

"I can't believe this." I look back at the photo, recognizing the faint scar on her left wrist. The night of the party, she told me she got it falling off her horse at a dressage competition. There's a gleam in her eyes that I remember, too, a spark that made me desperate to have her as my friend.

"Is she—does she know I'm—" My throat clogs, but Austin fills in the blanks.

"Yes," he says. "I reached out to her yesterday. She was happy you're doing well. She wanted to talk with you about what happened."

"She wants to talk to me." I can't believe this.

He squeezes my hand again. "It was her idea. She thought it could do you both some good."

"I never Googled her," I whisper. "I looked up Bridget once, and I felt so shitty when I saw she was in prison that I couldn't bear to take it any further."

"She's not angry," Austin says. "Marcella isn't. Not at you, not at anyone. I'll let her tell you the rest of it herself, but it's important you know that going in."

My eyes prickle with tears, and I take some deep breaths to keep from crying. I've spent thirteen years running from my past. Confronting it now should be scary, but it's not. Not like I thought it would be.

I look at Austin, and I know he's the reason.

He stares back at me, blue eyes steady and reassuring and so full of kindness I nearly collapse. But I don't. I hold myself up and take a deep breath.

"You ready?" he asks.

I nod. "Yes."

"It's time for some closure."

It's past time. Long past time.

With that, we turn and walk toward the coffee shop.

CHAPTER 17

AUSTIN

ours later, I hear the click of a key card in the hotel room door. I sit up fast, surprised to realize I dozed off while reviewing my presentation on statewide regulatory updates.

Here's hoping attendees don't do the same.

"Bree." I run a hand through my hair and watch her face as she walks through the door and across the dimly-lit hotel room. "How did it go?"

There are tear tracks on her cheeks, but her smile is like the sun coming out. "Oh, Austin."

The wobble in her voice isn't sadness or regret. It's relief. I'd know it anywhere, because that's what I'm feeling now.

I start to stand, to embrace her as she reaches the bed. But she drops down beside me and wraps her arms around my torso, burying her face against my chest. "Thank you," she murmurs into my shirt. "Thank you so much for everything."

Thank God.

I stroke her back, basking in my own relief. There were so many ways this could have gone wrong. Marcella could have been angry or judgmental, could have set Bree back to square one. But she wanted closure, too.

"It was good then." I slide my fingers through her curls as she burrows against me like an animal seeking warmth. She's such a force of nature that I forget how small she is. Having her curled against my chest like this is a reminder of how tiny she is.

"How did you know?" she asks.

I don't answer right away, not sure I understand the question. She draws back to look me in the eye, one hand flat on my chest. "How did you know that was exactly what I needed?"

"Talking with Marcella?"

She nods, circling her palm over my heart. "That, but also this. Touching you. Being held. Knowing you're there for me, even when I didn't know that's what I needed. That you're my rock."

"Always," I say, even though that's a bold thing to stay. I'm not even sure we're back together, so it's crazy to start promising forever.

But that's what I want, and her eyes tell me I'm not alone.

I stroke her hair again, loving the feel of those wild curls rippling through my fingers. "She said on the phone she always felt guilty," I tell her. "When I called to set up your meeting with her, Marcella told me she always hated that you went to juvey for something you didn't do."

"It wasn't her fault."

"She knows." Bree's palm on my chest is making the blood drain from my head to places it shouldn't be right now, and I'm determined not to be a creep. Not to take advantage of Bree's vulnerability. "She wanted you to hear that firsthand from her. To apologize for letting you take the fall."

"She didn't need to apologize," Bree says. "She told me I shouldn't apologize either, but we both needed to. I'm glad we did."

"Closure."

"Yes. The start of it, anyway." Her laugh shifts her body closer so her breast presses against my arm. "We talked about doing therapy together. It's not a bad idea."

"It could be helpful." I hold my breath, wondering if she knows what she's doing. That her palm is circling lower and lower, moving closer to my belt buckle. She shifts so her breasts sandwich my elbow, and I'm having trouble staying focused on the conversation.

She smiles like she's just read my thoughts. Her green eyes are clear and bright, with the last remnants of tears evaporating like the end of a rainstorm. That's not sadness I'm seeing in her expression. It's something else. Something I recognize deep in my gut.

And other parts.

"Bree." My breath catches as her fingers skim my belt buckle. "You don't have to—"

"I want to," she says. "I've never wanted anything as much as I want this right now."

Jesus.

She licks her lips, and it's all I can do to keep from lunging for her. "Do you want me?" she whispers.

"Yes." My voice is husky, barely my own. "So much."

And then we're kissing.

It happens so fast that I'm not sure who moves first. We collide like gravity's pulling us together, like we've been moving toward this moment for a thousand lifetimes.

I fall back onto the bed, not sure if I'm pulling her with me or if she pushed us into motion. She lands on my chest, the delicious, warm weight of her pressing me back against the mattress. God, she's sweet. Her mouth, her skin, everything about her tastes like raspberries and sunshine. I've never wanted anyone more than I want Bree right now.

I slide a hand up the back of her thigh to steady her and connect with bare skin. Her skirt rides up as she straddles me, groaning as she grinds against my fly. We're dry humping like a couple high school kids on prom night, and I ache with the urge to be inside her.

She draws back, and the heat in her eyes matches what's simmering in my chest right now. "Make love to me," she says. "Please don't make me wait, Austin."

God, the way she says my name.

And the way she's looking at me, with an urgent craving in her eyes and in her voice. It ignites the same thing in me, and my last shred of restraint falls to the floor like a blouse torn off.

I tug at the zipper on her skirt while Bree yanks at my belt. Shoes go flying, and shirts and socks. Never in the history of human clothing have two people gotten naked as quickly as we do. If this were a stripping contest, we'd get a gold medal.

Her breasts fall free from the lace bra, and I cup them in my hands, dizzy with the weight of them. She leans into my palms and kisses me, thighs splaying open as her slick heat connects with the dull throb between my legs.

"Condom," I groan, wondering where my pants went.

"On it." She reaches behind her like a sex magician and produces the prophylactic. She's got it on me before I can draw a full breath, and then she's on me.

And I'm in her and *oh, God.*

My hands grip her hips as she slides slick and tight around me. "Jesus, Bree."

She responds with a sound that's somewhere between a groan and a growl, hips moving with urgent need. She closes her eyes and tips her head back, curls falling around her shoulders. I watch her in wonder as her fingers slide down her chest and over her breasts, thumbs grazing her nipples.

Fuck, she's beautiful.

Beautiful and *mine.*

She's moving with a rhythm I swear I can hear, like a song I've known for years and still love. Her core clenches around me and I feel her body tense.

"That's it," I murmur. "Take what you need."

She opens her eyes and smiles, and my heart melts in a hot puddle. Her thumbs stroke her nipples, palms cupping the warm weight of her breasts. My hands rise to join them, fingers twining together as she slides down harder onto me.

"Austin," she groans. "I've never felt so—"

Her voice breaks in a moan, but I know the rest of that sentence. Not the exact words, but *this,* this thing between us that's like two souls spinning into one.

"You're so deep," she gasps. "So fucking good."

I'm gonna lose it. The sight of her touching herself, of our hands joined together on her breasts, the feeling of her slick heat around me, it's too much.

She tosses her curls, and I plunge right over the edge.

"Austin." Her eyes go wide and I know she's there with me. "Oh, God."

We explode together, a clenching, clutching frenzy of sensation. She's pulsing around me, gripping me tight as she rides each wave of shared pleasure. She throws her head back and screams, and I thank God I had the good sense to get a room on a different floor from my deputies. Not that I care. I'm so lost in pleasure, so lost in Bree, that I wouldn't mind if the whole fucking squad sat on the foot of the bed and watched.

She comes down slowly, her body heavy with concrete-filled limbs. I catch her as she falls, palms circling her ribcage as I pull us down onto the bed and roll so we're facing each other.

Bree opens her eyes and smiles. "I love you."

Holy shit.

There's a two-second delay while my brain processes the words and comes up with something smarter to say than *Are you fucking serious?*

"I love you, too." I push a damp curl off her forehead. "So much."

I've known for days, weeks even. But saying it out loud feels so good that I say it again. "I love you, Bree."

Her smile widens as I kiss her softly and slip my fingers into her hair. We kiss like that for a long time, bodies pressed so close we're touching at a thousand heated points.

She's still smiling when she breaks the kiss. "Can we start again?" she asks. "You and me, a clean slate."

"Always," I tell her, no hesitation at all. "We can always start again."

* * *

WE PULL into my driveway as the sky is turning pink and orange the next evening. Virginia bursts through the pet door doing her full-body wag, eager to inform me that Kim failed to offer unlimited kibble and a ribeye steak.

"It's good to see you, girl." I stoop down to scratch my pup behind the ears, but the traitor sets her sights on Bree. She scurries over and collapses at Bree's feet with her tongue lolling, thumping her tail on the gravel to punctuate her adoration.

Bree laughs. "Hey, you!" She kneels down and doles out belly rubs as Virginia telegraphs the message that this is her best day *ever*. "I'm glad to see you, too."

The sight of my dog and my girlfriend—holy shit, *my girlfriend*—slathering love on each other leaves me all warm and fuzzy, and I wonder what it would be like to do this every day. To come home to Bree and Virginia and hell, maybe a couple kids. I know this is all still new, but I can picture it like a television sitcom that's playing on repeat in my brain.

Bree stands up and I help her to her feet. "I'm going in to start the pork loin, but you're welcome to hang out with the dog," I say. "There's a Frisbee on the porch."

Virginia pants with approval, tail beating a rhythm on my shoe.

"Nah, I'll help with dinner." Bree falls into step beside me as Virginia trots between us, barking her enthusiasm.

I'm relieved when I unlock the front door and remember that I had the good sense to tidy up before I left town. Kim and Meredith took turns caring for my dog, and they've set my mail on the counter. Someone—Kim, probably—stuck a bunch of daisies in a vase on the table, and the smell of cinnamon suggests one of them baked cookies or burned a candle.

"I like your place," Bree says as she steps over the threshold. "It's really homey."

I hang my keys on the hook by the door as Virginia settles with a groan on her bed by the fireplace. "I didn't give you a proper tour before, did I?"

Bree's cheeks redden, and she glances away. "I guess my last visit was a little messed up, huh?"

"Come on." I catch her hand so she can't start down that path and pull her in for a quick kiss. "Let's do a fresh-start tour."

Bree smiles. "Deal."

I lead her around the cabin, pointing out the bathroom off the kitchen and the guest suite where Meredith stays each time she dumps a live-in boyfriend.

"This master bedroom is amazing." Bree trails a hand over the footboard of my massive log bed. "I like how you went with white and green and all the crisp pops of color instead of the red/gold thing most people do when they try for a rustic look."

I scan my bedroom through her eyes, not ashamed to admit I can picture us having sex on every surface. "I can't take credit for the decorating," I admit. "Kim's an interior designer. I hired her to do the whole place after I built it."

"It suits you." She presses a hand into the comforter, and I imagine myself tossing her back onto it and kissing my way up her body.

But there's time for that later.

"Let's start dinner." I slip my fingers through hers and lead her back down the hall. "Want a glass of wine?"

"I'd love one." She gives me a sheepish smile. "Still got the Pinot I brought?"

"Yep. Wine glasses are over there. Decanter, too, if you want to be fancy."

"No need for fancy." She sets to work uncorking the bottle while I turn and start pulling stuff out of the fridge.

"The pork won't take long," I tell her. "You okay with Caesar salad and roasted potatoes?"

"I can make the salad."

I pass her a cutting board and my good chef's knife while Bree finishes pouring the wine. She hands me a glass, and we set to work chopping and seasoning, our hands brushing each other's bodies each time we move past one another in the small space. I love how we work together. I love being here with the woman I love, making a meal to enjoy together. When I reach past her to flip on some music, Bree laughs and wiggles her hips to the beat.

God, I love her.

Once the pork is grilling, I steal a few seconds to check my phone. "Sorry." I flash Bree an apologetic look as I hit the keys to access my voicemail. "I haven't checked in since I left the conference, so I need to make sure there aren't any fires to put out."

"No problem," she says. "I should probably do the same thing, but I'm not ready to deal with my brothers."

I dial the code for my voicemail and the automatic voice reports the grim news.

You have six new messages.

I sigh and hit the button to hear the first one.

"Hello, Austin. This is Joan Sampson. About that calendar—"

I close my eyes and stifle a groan of frustration. When I open my eyes again, I notice the first couple lines of transcription for the next messages are pretty much the same. There's one from Mrs. Percy, too, and I scroll fast when I see the word "g-string." Two more from Mrs. Sampson, and then—

"Everything okay?"

I glance up to see Bree watching me with concern.

"Yeah," I mutter, scrolling to the final message. "Just my sixth grade teacher trying to get me naked again."

Bree laughs and goes back to chopping. "Can't say I blame her."

I sigh and scroll to the final message.

MESSAGE SIX.

"HEY, Austin! It's Aunt Genevieve. I've been trying to reach Bree, but her phone goes right to voicemail and her brother said she's with you. I have some exciting news about the show. Could you please have her call me?"

Whatever noise I make prompts Bree to look up again. "Still okay?"

"More than okay. Here." I dial Genevieve's number, then put the call on speaker. It rings twice before Aunt Gen picks up.

"Austin," she says. "Please tell me you've got that beautiful girl somewhere close by."

"I'm assuming you mean Bree." I grin and slide an arm around Bree as she eyes me curiously. "She's right here, and you're on speakerphone."

"Hello, Genevieve." Bree snuggles closer, and I'm distracted by all that heat and softness. "It's great to hear your voice."

"Oh, this is perfect," Gen says. "I get to tell you both at the same time."

Bree glances at me and bites her lip. "Tell us what?"

"I just got out of a meeting with the executive team," she says. "They want to start filming in three weeks. We'll do segments on Ponderosa Luxury Ranch Resort and on Jingle Bell Reindeer Ranch, too. The producers are thrilled to get it into the lineup so fast."

Bree squeals and throws her arms around my neck. Her body feels unreal pressed up against mine, and I remind myself to send Aunt Gen a thank you note.

"Oh my God." Bree bounces in my arms, and I'm treated to the delicious sway of her breasts against my ribs. "This is amazing. I can't wait to talk to Jade and Amber."

"I called them about ten minutes ago," Gen says. "I swore them to secrecy, so I could call you myself."

"You don't know how much this means to me." Bree is beaming, her green eyes lit with excitement. "To us—my brothers and me."

"We're excited, too," she says. "I'm shooting you an email with the production schedule. It'll be a mix of obvious things like the spa and the wedding site, plus local flavor. I'd love to get your ideas there."

"You mean footage of things around town?" she asks.

"Exactly," she says. "We want to capture the whole small-town vibe."

"The Dandelion Café is cute," Bree says. "You could get some B-roll at one of the breweries or downtown on Art Hop night."

"How about the cupcake shop?" I suggest, wanting to be helpful.

"Good thinking," Bree says. "I'm sure Chelsea would be up for it."

"We're looking for quirky things, too," Gen adds. "Charming little details like a high school football game or a charity bake sale —that kind of thing."

Bree gives me a look I can't quite read, then winks. "How about a charity calendar featuring photos of local cops?"

Aunt Gen laughs. "Oh, that's perfect. I'll have my secretary get in touch with some meeting times and we can schedule a brainstorming call in the next couple days."

Wait, what?

I'm still gaping at her as they say their goodbyes and hang up. I pull her into my arms, too happy for Bree to be annoyed about the calendar thing. "Congratulations. I know this is a big deal for you."

"I'm so happy." She bounces a little in my arms. "I never would have met her without you, so I owe you big-time."

I palm her ass and grin. "My pleasure."

She giggles and lifts up on tiptoes to kiss me. "This is amazing."

I lose myself in the kiss for a few seconds before remembering the tail end of the conversation. With my sternest cop stare, I pull back and squeeze her butt a little harder. "Did you have to mention the damn calendar?"

Laughing, she slings a leg around my waist and pulls me against her so I'm pressed against her core. "Still not a fan of stripping for a good cause?"

"I'm all for taking my clothes off," I say, grinding into her. "Just not for the townspeople or a bunch of old ladies. I don't want other cops turned into sex objects, either."

"I hear you loud and clear." She gives me a mock salute. "From now on, you're just my sex object."

"That's more like it." I kiss her again, sliding a hand up to cup her breast. "So why the hell did you mention the calendar to Aunt Gen?"

"Because I have an idea for how to do it better," she says. "This is part of my new self-improvement plan. Bree-two-point-oh solves problems instead of running from them."

My thumb skims her nipple through the thin cotton of her

shirt, distracting us both for a second. "I like all versions of Bree," I tell her. "But I'd prefer whichever one is going to get me out of posing for a lecherous calendar."

"No lecherous posing," she assures me, doing something extra-lecherous as she slides a hand into the front of my pants. "You can keep your clothes on and everything."

"For the calendar," I clarify.

"Only for the calendar," she assures me as I back her up until she bumps the counter, threading my fingers through her curls. "I have other plans for your immediate future."

I can't wait. Not just for the immediate future, but the one that comes after that. The long-term future, which I know involves Bree and me together. I can feel it.

I can also feel her unzipping my fly as I boost her up on the counter. "I'm really loving your ideas," I tell her. "And I love the hell out of you."

"And I love you, Sergeant Sexypants," she says, shoving my jeans down over my hips. "Pants or no pants."

"Let's go with no pants."

She giggles and tilts her head back to kiss me. "Deal."

EPILOGUE

BREE

"*T*hat tux is *everything*." I tug the lapels of Austin's powder-blue suit and pull him down for a kiss.

Holy yum, I'll never get tired of this.

We're both grinning when we pull back, and I wonder if he knows I'm hanging on to his tuxedo jacket for balance. After all these months, I still get dizzy when we kiss like that.

"Hey, sexy." He kisses me again, softer this time, but every bit as mind-blowing.

"Hey, Chief Hottie." I let go of his jacket and smooth out the front of it. "I still can't believe you found this thing in a thrift store." Sliding my hands down and around, I cup his butt through his dress pants and give a squeeze.

"Hands off, kids." Jade King zips past and swats my knuckles with a ruler—not hard, but enough to send a loud *thwap* across the ballroom. She grins at me and keeps moving. "We need one phone book's width between your bodies at all times," she add. "No hanky-panky."

Brandon laughs behind her, knowing damn well hanky-panky is on everyone's mind. It's kinda the point of having an old-school eighties prom for guests over twenty-one. He throws me a wink as he trails after his fiancée, looking every bit the prom king in his ruffle-front shirt and bowtie.

"I think she's letting the prom supervisor thing go to her head," he tells me, patting Jade's butt beneath the massive teal bow at the back of her dress. "I'm diggin' it."

Jade turns her ruler on him with a saucy glint in her eye, and I silently congratulate myself for appointing her our official prom monitor. The role suits her.

Brandon scoops her up in a swirl of laughter and hauls her toward a corner of the room, possibly to reprimand more prom-goers, but more likely to make out in a closet. They're almost out of sight when Brandon turns and gives Austin a discreet thumbs-up.

Huh?

He pulls me into his arms again, distracting me by wrapping his fingers up in the laces at the back of my dress while Cyndi Lauper croons about girls wanting to have fun. I can relate. Honestly though, I can't remember ever having this much fun with my clothes on. These last few months have been the best of my life.

"I get to undo these later, right?" Austin murmurs in my ear as he tugs at the strings holding my dress together in back. "Or now. Now's good."

I laugh and nudge his hand away before he can do any serious unraveling. "I know the corset-back isn't technically eighties, but this is the prom dress I always wanted," I admit a little sheepishly. "I figure I could fudge a little."

"Honey, you can do whatever you want, since you planned the damn event. And since you're raising a gazillion dollars for chari-ty." He lowers his mouth to my ear again, swaying to the music. "And since you look like a fucking wet dream in this dress."

I smile as he twirls me around, spinning me so my belly somersaults as I scan the crowd. Holy cow, half the town must be here. "It really is a nice turnout."

I'm being modest, but I'm so damn proud I could explode. Hundreds of bodies sway together under the swirl of disco lights. Everyone's drinking and laughing and busting out their best breakdance moves as the song shifts to a Michael Jackson hit. Half the people in this room probably wore diapers when this song was popular, but they're having a great time.

I'm part of this. I made it happen.

Friends. Community.

And yeah, awesome sex—all of that is finally mine.

Austin smiles like he knows what I'm thinking. He probably does. The guy is practically a mind reader, but that's not a bad thing. He kisses my temple. "Between the fact that everyone paid eighty bucks a head to get in, and the fact that you're donating all the proceeds from food and drink sales—"

"And the photo booth," I remind him.

"That, too." He twirls me again. "It's hands down the biggest fundraiser the Deschutes Children's Welfare Society has ever seen."

I smile as we slip into a quick shuffle-step. Austin's a surprisingly good dancer. He's good at lots of things, all of which I've loved discovering over the last few months.

"I can't believe they managed to make our ballroom look like a freakin' gymnasium," I tell him. "Remind me to get pictures in case I ever have a bride who wants an eighties theme."

"You outdid yourself, Miss Bracelyn," he tells me. "Congratulations."

I'm saved from my urge to blush when Mrs. Sampson rushes up, calendar in hand. "Austin, dear." She thrusts a Sharpie at him, and I resist the temptation to make a crack about anti-graffiti laws and permanent markers in public places. "Will you sign my calendar?"

"Absolutely." He flips the cover of *Cops and Critters*, and there's that bubble of pride again. This was my brainchild, my way of appeasing the ladies, supporting the Humane Society, and oh yeah, keeping the officers fully-clothed. All the cops are posed with their pets, and the proceeds go to the local animal shelter.

"We've already sold more than three hundred," Mrs. Sampson says proudly as Austin scrawls his name below his picture on the September page. "What a great idea using this dance as the kickoff event for it."

"I'm so glad it worked out," I tell her, lowering my voice to a conspiratorial whisper. "Don't tell anyone I said so, but Austin and Virginia's picture is the cutest."

"Oh, I know it, honey." She pretends to fan herself as Austin recaps the pen and hands it back to her with the calendar.

"Let me know if you want Virginia Woof to pawtograph it for you later," he quips. "All this fame is going to her head."

Mrs. Sampson titters and tucks the calendar under her arm. "As soon as we do another print run, I'll buy more for all my grandchildren."

We watch as she hustles away, vanishing into the crowd of dancers. I look up at Austin and smirk. "Just a guess, but I'm thinking she wouldn't buy it for her grandkids if it had naked pictures of you holding your cop hat over your junk."

"Let's hope not."

I do a little pirouette to make my dress shimmer around me, then twirl back into the safety of Austin's arms as the music shifts to a slow dance. Bon Jovi, I think. "Did I tell you we booked two more weddings this morning? That's eight since the episode trailers started running."

"I saw one last night when I was watching the news." Austin grins. "Pretty wild to see my hometown in commercials for a famous wedding program. You're gonna kill it when the show airs."

"That's the hope. I couldn't have done it without you."

"Sure you could have." He smiles and spins me again. "You can do anything you set your mind to."

With you I can. I think it, but don't say it, because duh, that's cheesy.

But I think he knows it. We spend almost every waking hour together when we're not working, and like I said about the mind reader thing.

Austin draws me back against his chest as Sean approaches with a silver platter of shrimp ceviche bites in one hand. My brother is dapper in a hideous silver tux and a resigned look that I know is only a cover for the fact that he's loving this almost as much as I am. Beside him, Amber is resplendent in a poofy-sleeved pink gown.

"Here." Sean thrusts the tray at us. "Hurry up and eat the last of these so I can put the damn tray down and go make out in the backseat of a Gremlin or something."

"How about a vintage Volvo?" Austin grabs one of the ceviche bites. "I have it on good authority the seats tilt back nicely."

I flush with the memory as Amber rolls her eyes. "No car sex," she says. "Yet. I'm holding out for a slow dance to an eighties ballad. 'Careless Whisper,' or maybe 'True.'"

"How about Poison doing 'Talk Dirty to Me?'" Sean suggests.

Amber pretends to consider it. "That'll do."

I grab a couple more shrimp bites and set one on Austin's plate. "A slow dance for a trip to second base," he muses. "That seems fair."

Shoveling in a mouthful of shrimp ceviche, I make yummy noises at my brother. "Thanks for playing waiter," I tell him. "I've had four different people gush at me about meeting the famous chef."

"It's been fun," he admits. "Except the part where some old lady tried to stuff a handful of ones in my pants."

Austin cringes, and I know what he's thinking. *Mrs. Sampson.*

I glance across the room and see her making a beeline for James. My brother's wearing a pained expression and an Armani tux that's totally not eighties, but I doubt anyone notices. He's distinguished and handsome and totally out of his element.

It's good for him.

Mrs. Sampson gives his tie a flirty yank and says something that makes him step back. I should probably go save him, but James is a big boy. He can handle himself.

I glance back to see Amber's watching him, too. "Lawyer Boy needs someone to spike his punch."

Sean and I both laugh. "You have someone in mind for the job?" I ask.

"I might." Amber tosses her poofy ponytail and smiles. "You've met my friend, Lily?"

The word *man-eater* floats through my head, but I bite my tongue. "The one in the painted-on silver-sequined dress that looks like a zillion bucks?"

"That's her." Amber plucks another ceviche bite off Sean's platter. "Let's talk TV. Has your phone been ringing off the hook since the commercials started airing?"

"It's insane." I smile up at Austin, who just exchanged a funny look with Sean and mouthed something I couldn't make out. What the heck?

"I love that one clip of the reindeer at the wedding ceremony." I focus on Amber, ignoring the fact that the guys are acting odd. "And that candid shot of Jade and Brandon kissing by the barn."

"Oh, she *hates* that." Amber laughs. "At least she says she does."

We both know better, which is awesome. Not just that Jade's so happy, though that's awesome, too. I love having a clique, having these girlfriend relationships where we read each other's undercurrents. It's something I always wished for.

Amber's still talking, so I order myself to stop being a socially-awkward dork and pay attention. "Besides landing a bunch of weddings, we've already booked the reindeer for five new holiday appearances in December."

"Hope you don't run out of reindeer," Austin says.

"Funny you say that." Amber snags another shrimp bite. "Jade's talking about adopting two more from some rescue place in Eastern Oregon, just to make sure we've got enough. I swear, your aunt is a hero."

I smile and reach up to tug Austin's tie. "Remind me to send flowers to Genevieve."

"You can give them to her in person," he says. "She'll be at dinner next week."

See? That's what I mean. I'm part of a family now, part of a community. I love that I go to his parents' place for holidays, and that he joins my brothers and me for dinner at the resort. We've woven ourselves into each other's families, and it's hard to imagine we weren't always part of the fabric of each other's lives.

"Hey, guys." Chelsea from Dew Drop Cupcakes sidles up with a tray of mini treats and waves it under our noses. "I've got chocolate with lavender buttercream and lime with toasted meringue. Help me out so I can get home and relieve the babysitter."

A little ripple of disappointment runs through me. "You're not sticking around to dance?"

"'Fraid not." Chelsea blows her teased-up bangs off her forehead. "The kiddo had a tummy ache earlier this week, so I'll feel better if I'm home. Amy's covering me here for the rest of the night."

"That's too bad," I say, hoping I sound suitably sympathetic about the kid. "I was hoping you could meet my brother."

"Hello." Sean lifts his brows. "What am I, chopped liver?"

"She already knows you, dummy." I slug him in the arm. "I meant Mark."

Amber pretends to stagger with astonishment. "Mark's coming? To an eighties prom? In public?"

"Not technically," I admit. "But I was thinking I could break something and he'd have to come fix it."

Chelsea laughs and pops a mini cupcake onto everyone's plate. "Some other time. Gotta run."

She hustles away, followed by Sean and Amber, which leaves me alone with Austin. He gives me a raised eyebrow before pulling me against his chest. "Promise me you're not match-making your grumpy, burly brother with a sweet cupcake peddler," he says.

"I'll promise no such thing," I tell him. "I only make promises I'm positive I can keep."

"Good to know." The words rumble through him, sending soft vibrations against my chest. We sway together under the twirling lights, our bodies fitted together like we're molded out of clay. When Austin speaks again, there's a surprising tenderness in his voice. "Is this everything you wanted it to be?"

The prom.

He means the prom, but maybe that's not all he means. "It's better than I expected." I pull back to look at him, needing him to understand I mean all of this. Him, me, the two of us together. "It's so much better than I ever imagined I'd have."

He smiles, and I know he gets it. "I'm glad. So damn glad."

I snuggle into him again, closing my eyes as we sway to the music. When the ballad starts to fade, I open my eyes to see Jade and Brandon standing next to the small stage at the other end of the room.

Did Austin just nod at them?

I draw back to study him, but he's got the perfect poker face. "What?"

"Nothing. I just—"

Screeeeeeeeech!

A microphone's shriek bounces off the ballroom walls, halting the final notes of Madonna crooning "Crazy for You." I jerk back and turn to see Brandon hopping onto the stage, mike in his hand.

"Good evening, ladies and gentleman," he says. "Thank you all for coming to the first annual Kids and Critters Eighties Prom. Everyone having a great time?"

Wait, what?

"This isn't on the agenda," I whisper. Glancing up, I see Austin's not the least bit alarmed. In fact, he looks—excited? Nervous?

What on earth is happening?

There's a clatter of enthusiastic applause, and I turn my attention back to the stage. Hold on, is that Sean and James and—wait, *Mark?*— off to the side looking obnoxiously smug?

Up on stage, Brandon shifts the mike to his other hand. "It's time to announce this year's prom king and queen."

Jade walks across the stage to join him, holding a red velvet pillow topped with a sparkly tiara that resembles one my mother made me wear to a cotillion years ago. Beside it is a crown that looks just as old. Didn't Austin say Brandon was their class's prom king?

Brandon shoots us a wink and continues. "Austin Dugan and Bree Bracelyn, will you come up here?"

I gasp. I can't help it. This can't be happening.

One look at Austin tells me it's not only happening, he's behind it.

Oh my God.

"Come on." Austin grins and pulls me toward the stage as my heart thuds in my ears.

It's silly to be so excited. I know that, but I still am. It's not like I harbor some teenage fantasy of being prom queen, but it's the idea of it. The thought I belong. That I matter enough for someone to go to this kind of trouble for *me.*

My legs wobble as we mount the steps to the stage. A cluster of helium balloons bobs up from behind the speakers. Blue and gold, red and white, they float into the air amid gasps of surprised delight from the crowd.

I still can't figure out what's happening, but I love it. I want to record every second to watch over and over when I catch myself feeling like my scared, friendless teenage self. I glance at my brothers again to see Sean holding a video recorder. He gives me a thumbs-up, then makes a shooing motion to focus my attention back to the stage.

"Wow, this is such an honor," Austin's saying, and I realize he's holding the mike now. How did that happen?

He crouches down so Jade can put the crown on his head before she slides sideways and secures my tiara in place. Then she squeezes my arm and steps back.

Austin smiles and continues. "Can't claim I'm too qualified to be a prom king, but everyone in this room who's met Bree knows she's already a queen."

More applause echoes through the room as my heart swells, and my eyes fill with tears. I swallow hard, wondering when my throat closed up. Not that I'd have any idea what to say right now.

Austin lets go of my hand. The second he reaches into his jacket pocket, *I know*. I know what's happening here.

Oh my God.

"Prom night might be a weird time to do this," he says, offering me an awkward smile. "I promise this isn't a shotgun kinda thing."

There's a ripple of laughter in the front row, but my eyes are fixed on Austin's face. I'm dimly aware of the ring box, but that's not what I care about. What I care about most is the look in his eyes right now. It's a look that says we belong together, forever and ever, the two of us.

I know because I'm feeling it, too.

"Bree Bracelyn," he says. "I'm madly, passionately, crazily in love with you."

He drops to one knee, and a tear slips down my cheek. I always told myself I wouldn't be one of those sobbing women if someone proposed to me. I'd be serene and composed and joyful, but I can't seem to stop the tears leaking from the edges of my eyes.

"You're crazy," I whisper, and my voice comes out on a sob. "I love you so much."

There's a flicker of relief in his eyes, and I realize what it took for him to do this. Sure, we've talked about marriage—*duh*—but putting himself out there like this. Taking a public risk.

If it's possible, I love him more now than I did thirty seconds ago.

I'm smiling so hard my cheeks hurt as Austin sets the mike on the floor beside him and opens the ring box. Something sparkly is inside, but I can't see it through the tears. That's fine, it's not the ring that matters.

"You're the most amazing woman I've ever met, and I can't imagine the rest of my life without you in it," he continues. "Marry me, Bree. Be my queen forever."

He hardly gets the words pasts his lips before I'm choking out a response. "Yes," I sob as another tear slips down my cheek. "Oh my God, *yes*." I nod so hard the tiara slips off my head, but he catches it in one hand.

The other hand's still gripping the ring box, so he sets the tiara on the floor next to the mike and slips the ring on my finger. A perfect fit. I blink hard to clear my vision and realize it's something vintage. Oh my God, his grandmother's ring? His mom showed it to me at Thanksgiving when we sat with his sisters to paw through her old jewelry box. I played it cool, but it was all I could do not to fall over myself blathering about how beautiful it was, how lucky they were to have family memories like that.

Austin stands up and puts the tiara back on my head. The crowd's applauding now, but I can hardly hear over the roar in my head. All I can see is Austin, the love in his eyes, the smile on his face.

He's going to be my husband.

I throw both arms around his neck and pull him down for a kiss so passionate I see stars flickering in front of my eyes. Or maybe that's the confetti.

"Austin." I draw back to flutter a hand through the shreds of colorful paper and glittery bits falling around us. "How did you pull this off?"

He grins and kisses me again. "That's the nice thing about being a small-town cop. Lots of connections to good people."

I wiggle my finger in front of me, thrilled to see that ring on my finger. Thrilled to be in Austin's arms. Thrilled to realize this is my life. Friendless Bree Bracelyn—who'd have thought?

I twine my hands around his neck as someone ducks close for a photo. "So this is what I was missing out on with my no-cops rule."

He laughs and tips his chin down, brushing my lips with his as the crowd cheers. "Here's to a lifetime of breaking rules together."

* * *

READY FOR MARK and Chelsea's story? That's next in the Ponderosa Resort Romantic Comedy Series, and you can grab it right here:

Hottie Lumberjack

books2read.com/u/mZP6QB

Keep reading for a sneak peek at the opening scene from *Hottie Lumberjack* . . .

YOUR EXCLUSIVE SNEAK PEEK AT
HOTTIE LUMBERJACK

CHELSEA

"*H*ere you go, Mrs. Sampson." I slide the pink bakery box across the counter with a smile. "One dozen Guinness chocolate cupcakes with chai spice frosting, and one dozen strawberry with vanilla fondant."

My retired math teacher pulls the box to her chest like she thinks someone will snatch it. "Did you put the penises on top like I asked?"

Her volume is a good indication she forgot her hearing aid, and the chime of my front door is a good indication of how my week's going. I order myself to stay focused on the customer in front of me, but from the corner of my eye I see the new arrival flinch in surprise.

"I'll be with you in just a—*oh*."

Holy shit.

The guy in the doorway of my bakery doesn't look like someone shopping for a dozen vanilla bean cupcakes. He looks like a lumberjack who lost his way to the forest. The scruffy beard, the plaid flannel, and ohmygod is that an *axe*?

I swallow hard and glance at Mrs. Sampson, reminding myself not to alarm her. If we're going to die at the hands of an axe murderer, I'd like her to go out knowing she got what she wanted in that bakery box. "The cupcakes are made to order, just like always," I assure her. "I even slipped in a couple complimentary macarons because I know Mr. Sampson loves them."

She frowns but doesn't turn around to notice the hulking figure behind her. "But the penises," she says. "They're for a bachelorette party for my grand-niece and—"

"You've got your penises." I wince at the sharpness of my words, wishing desperately we could stop saying that word in front of a guy who presumably has one. I'm trying not to look. "And I've got your order for next week's Welfare Society luncheon. Can I get you anything else, Mrs. Sampson?"

"No, dear," she says, finally convinced that I successfully piped one dozen flesh-colored phalluses onto her pastries. "You're a doll, Chelsea. I hope you find a man soon."

As if that weren't embarrassing enough, she reaches across the counter and pats my cheek. Then she turns and brushes past the man who's looking more than a little regretful about walking in here.

I get a better look at him this time, and nope, I didn't imagine the axe. Or the fact that he has to be at least six-five, which means he has to duck to get under the doorframe as he holds it open for Mrs. Sampson.

"Ma'am." His voice is gruff, but his eyes are kind. "You need help getting that into your car?"

"Thank you, Mark," she says. "I've got it. You tell that sister of yours hello."

"Yes, ma'am."

Sister? Mark?

I study the guy more closely but see zero resemblance to five-foot-nothing Bree Bracelyn, the marketing VP for Ponderosa Ranch Luxury Resort. But this has to be the brother she's talked about for months, right?

The door swings shut and Paul Bunyan—er, Mark—turns to

face me. He scrubs a hand over his beard as he ambles toward the counter. "I need cupcakes."

I glance at the axe in his hand and nod. "Uh, you're in the right place for that."

Folding my hands on the counter, I meet his eyes. They're a warm brown like my favorite Guittard chocolate, and I forget for a moment that he could crush my skull with his hands if he wanted to. He doesn't appear to want to, but I don't have a history of being a great judge of men.

I push aside dark thoughts about my daughter's sperm donor and the half-dozen other men in my past who've turned out to be real doozies and focus on the more immediate threat. Or is there a threat? Hottie Lumberjack doesn't look terribly menacing. There's an odd sort of teddy bear quality to the guy, if teddy bears had massive biceps and broad shoulders and sharp pieces of weaponry in their paws.

He catches me staring and sets the axe down beside my display case, leaning it against his thigh. That's huge, too. Everything about this guy is enormous, so why do I feel more turned on than terrified?

The guy clears his throat. "I'm supposed to order two dozen cupcakes for a bunch of tour operators from—"

"I'm sorry, why do you have the axe?"

He cocks his head, genuinely perplexed. "For chopping wood."

For fuck's sake. "I mean why did you bring it into a cupcake shop?"

I'm no longer worried he's here to lop my head off, but still.

He stares at me for a few beats, not answering, not blinking, not even smiling. Not that I could tell, what with the thick beard masking any sort of expression. But I can see his lips, which are full and soft and—

"Sharp."

I blink. "What?"

"The axe," he says. "Had to get it sharpened."

"So you brought it to a cupcake shop?"

The corners of his mouth twitch, but he doesn't smile. "No, I brought it to the shop down the street. Didn't want to leave it in the truck because the doors don't lock. Safety hazard."

"Oh." That actually makes sense.

Sort of. If this is really Bree Bracelyn's brother, he's a freakin' gazillionaire. Not that any of the siblings in that family act like it, but it's common knowledge the Bracelyn kids inherited a lot more than their dad's ranch when he died.

Suffice it to say, Hottie Lumberjack could afford a truck that locks.

"Chelsea Singer," I tell him, wiping a hand on my pink and green striped apron before offering it to him. "I own Dew Drop Cupcakes." As an afterthought, I add, "And I'm not an axe murderer."

His mouth definitely twitches this time. "Mark Bracelyn. Ponderosa Resort. Also not an axe murderer."

"Good. That's good." And interesting. He didn't volunteer his job title, but I know it's something like Vice President of Grounds Management, which Bree told me he *hates*. He might be part-owner of a luxury resort for rich people, but he'd rather be regarded as the handyman. That's what Bree says, anyway.

And don't think I haven't noticed Bree filling my head with Mark-related tidbits.

Mark built me a new woodshed this weekend.

Mark has a major sweet tooth.

Mark rescued a family of orphaned bunnies yesterday.

I'm not sure whether she wants me to date him or just think twice about macing him if we meet in a dark alley, but it's odd this is the first time we're meeting.

"So Mark," I say, leaning against the counter. "What can I get for you?"

"Cupcakes." He frowns. "Two dozen."

"Right, but any particular flavor? Strawberry, peanut butter, kiwi, red velvet, double-fudge—" I stop when I see the dazed look in his eyes and nudge a laminated menu across the counter at him. "We have more than fifty cake flavors and three dozen frosting varieties, plus fondant and icing. There's an infinite variety of combinations."

Those brown eyes take on the ultimate "kid in a candy shop" glow, so I give him a private moment while I turn and wash my hands at the sink. His eyes become saucers as I turn back and reach into the display case to pull out a tray of mini cupcakes. I wouldn't do this for every customer, but Ponderosa Resort is one of my biggest clients.

"This is one of our seasonal favorites right now," I explain as I pluck a soft baby cupcake off the tray. "It's Guinness chocolate, and it's great with the Irish cream frosting. Would you like to try it?"

"Yes." His throat moves as he swallows. "Yes, please."

The gruff eagerness in his voice makes my girl parts clench, which is ridiculous. And a sign of how long it's been since I had sex, which….um, yeah. Let's just say dating's not easy for single moms.

I whip out a pastry bag and do a quick swirl of frosting on top of the cupcake. "Here you go."

Our fingers touch as I hand it across the counter, and I suppress an involuntary shiver. The good kind of shiver, like the one I do every time I bite into a perfect snickerdoodle. Good Lord, this guy has massive hands. He makes my mini cupcake look like a chocolate chip. "See what you think of that."

I have to look away from the expression of rapture on his face. There's something raw and intimate about it, and my belly's doing silly somersaults under my apron. I survey my tray, trying to come up with another good flavor combo.

"Let's see, this is one of Bree's favorites." I steal a look at his face, but if he's surprised I connected the dots to his sister, he doesn't show it. He's too fixated on his cupcake, savoring every little mini-bite like it's an act of worship.

This shouldn't be getting me hot, right?

I clear my throat and swirl some lime zest frosting onto a lemon cupcake. "Bree likes the citrus combo," I tell him. "Is it a family thing?"

Something odd flashes in his eyes, but he takes the mini cupcake and nods. "Thank you."

He eats this one more gingerly, still savoring every crumb. I glance down at the sample tray and try to think of what other flavors to offer. What would a guy like Mark Bracelyn enjoy? I don't make manly-man confections like sawdust cupcakes with drizzles of pine sap or mini-cakes infused with hints of leather and charcoal briquette. But maybe something on the other end of the spectrum.

"These tend to be too sweet for some people, but—"

"Yes." He nods. "Yes, please, I'd like to try it."

I smile and pluck a gooey-looking confection off the edge of the tray. "You're in luck, I had some left over from a kids' birthday party order. This is my coconut caramel chocolate delight cupcake. It's like those Girl Scout cookies—Samoas?—but in cupcake form."

The sheer joy in this man's eyes is enough to make my hand shake as I place it in the center of his massive palm. He lifts it to his mouth, and I swear on my KitchenAid mixer, I have a mini-orgasm. If the way to a man's heart is through his stomach, the way into my pants is through a man's sweet tooth.

What? No, I didn't just think that.

Holy shit, Chelsea, get it together.

I smooth out my apron as Mr. Tall, Gruff, and Silent polishes off his cupcake. I consider offering him more—cupcakes, not sexual favors—but what's that expression about free milk and cow buying and—

Great, now I'm thinking about Mark Bracelyn's hands on a pair of udders, which sooooo shouldn't be hot, but it is.

Stop it.

I clear my throat. "So what'll it be?" I ask. "You didn't mention when you need the order, but I have several of these in stock. Most will take a couple days, though."

Mark wipes his beard with a sleeve, and I realize I should have offered a napkin. He doesn't seem to need one, though, and his beard is remarkably crumb-free. What's it like to kiss a guy with facial hair? I've only experienced five-o-clock shadow, the sort of sandpaper scruff that leaves your cheeks raw and red. But Mark's beard looks soft, with hints of cinnamon and nutmeg.

Stop thinking of this man as edible.

"I'll take four dozen, please," he says.

I bite my lip, not positive I've got that much stock. "I thought Bree only needed two dozen."

"She does," he says. "The extras are for me. A dozen of whatever you've got in stock now, and the rest can wait 'til Friday."

I smile and jot the order on a notepad. "Got it. You want anything specific, or a mixed batch?"

He doesn't smile, but there's a flicker of interest in his eyes. "Surprise me."

Oh, baby.

"How about any pupcakes?" I offer.

Mark frowns. "Pupcakes?"

"Cupcakes for dogs," I say. For some reason I just assumed he has a dog. He looks like the sort of guy who'd have a Rottweiler or maybe a blue ox named Babe. "Bree buys them all the time for Virginia Woof."

"I should get a dog." He says this with an earnestness that makes my heart go gooey.

"You totally should." Good Lord, why am I advising this man on his life choices? "The Humane Society has tons of great ones. My daughter and I volunteer there every Saturday."

This is where most guys check out. Or check my ring finger. Or ask some not-so-subtle question about the baby-daddy, even though everyone pretends not to care. Plenty of folks have heard rumors.

But Mark doesn't blink. Just looks me in the eye, calm and steady. "Good idea."

"Which? Volunteering at the Humane Society, or you getting a dog."

"Yes."

I wait for more, but there doesn't seem to be any. His attention shifts to something over my shoulder, and he points one enormous finger. "How long's that been like that?"

I look where he's pointing and see the banged-up handle on the side door leading to the alley. I left it open a few inches to let the spring breeze waft through, and it's obvious even from here that someone messed with the doorknob.

"A couple days." I turn back to face him. "I came in the other morning and found it like that. Probably kids messing around. I haven't had time to call the repair guy."

Mark frowns. "May I?"

I'm not sure what he's asking, but I nod like an idiot. "Sure."

He lumbers around the counter, leaving his axe behind. After a few seconds of fiddling with the lock and muttering, he marches back around the counter. "Wait here."

"I—"

The front door swings shut behind him before I can point out that I've got no place to go, owning the shop and everything. He's not gone more than a minute, and when he strides back through the door, he's carrying a battered red toolbox.

He doesn't ask this time. Just rounds the corner and goes to the door again. There's some hammering and rattling, a few curse words that make me glad it's a slow weekday and there are no other customers around. I busy myself filling a bakery box with cupcakes, slipping in two extras and one of my cupcake-shaped business cards with a few words scrawled on the back.

Then I wander toward the door, watching his shoulders bunch as he works. He's rolled up the sleeves of his flannel shirt, revealing forearms thick and ropey with muscle. The man is huge, even kneeling on my floor.

I don't realize how close I've crept until he turns his head and—

"Um," he says.

He's face-to-boob with me, and we're frozen in the moment. I could step forward and feel the tickle of his beard against my breasts through the front of my T-shirt. He could lean in and whisper warm breath against my nipples, making them pucker through the lace of my bra.

But neither of us does that.

He's first to lift his gaze, meeting my eyes through a haze that looks like the same thing buzzing through my brain. "You're good."

"What?"

"The door." He gestures with a screwdriver but doesn't break eye contact. "That should hold now. No need to call a repairman."

I drag my eyes from his and see he's fixed my damn door. How about that?

"Wow." I step back at last, aware of the dizzy hum pulsing through my core. "That's—wow. What do I owe you?"

Mark stands and hoists his toolbox, wiping a hand on his jeans. "You gave me cupcake samples."

"Maybe a dollar's worth of samples," I point out. "A repairman would charge at least a hundred."

"You can give me a pupcake," he says. "When I get my dog."

He gives me a small smile, but I don't think he's kidding. I do think he's considering kissing me. I want him to, Jesus God, I want him to, and it's the craziest thing ever.

But he turns and lumbers back around the counter. Setting

down the toolbox, he fishes into his pocket and comes up with a battered leather wallet. "For the four-dozen cupcakes," he says, laying four hundred-dollar bills on the counter as my jaw falls open.

How much does this man think I charge for butter and sugar and—

"It was good meeting you." He gathers his axe and toolbox and the pink bakery box, then lumbers toward the door before I can muster any words like "wait" or "your receipt" or "please bend me over the counter."

The door swings shut behind him, and seconds later, a truck engine growls to life. I realize my mouth is still hanging open, so I close it and watch a faded blue and white pickup rumble down the street.

What the hell just happened?

***

Want to keep reading? You can nab Hottie Lumberjack here:
Hottie Lumberjack
books2read.com/u/mZP6QB

DON'T MISS OUT!

Want access to exclusive excerpts, behind-the-scenes stories about my books, cover reveals, and prize giveaways? Not only will you get all that by subscribing to my newsletter, but I'll even throw you a **FREE** short story featuring a swoon-worthy marriage proposal for Sean and Amber from *Chef Sugarlips*.

Get it right here.

http://tawnafenske.com/subscribe/

ACKNOWLEDGMENTS

I owe huge debts of gratitude to Fenske's Frisky Posse for all the eagle-eyed reads, amazing reviews, and general cheerleading. You guys are the awesomest street team in the history of street teams (here's where you gently point out that "awesomest" isn't a word).

Much love to Kait Nolan for all the self-pub coaching and long-distance tea and wine drinking parties, not to mention sleeping with me in Denver.

Huge, humongous, ENORMOUS love to Linda Grimes for all the amazing feedback. Can I have your next book now?!?!

Thank you to Meah Meow for being the best combination author assistant/pet sitter/all-around awesome person I know. I couldn't do this without you!

Much love and thanks to Susan Bischoff and Lauralynn Elliott of The Forge for all your hard work whipping this bad boy into shape. I'm also super-grateful to Lori Jackson Design for the fantastic teaser graphics, banners, and bookmarks.

Love and gratitude to my family, Aaron "Russ" Fenske and Carlie Fenske (and Paxton now, too!) and Dixie and David Fenske for always being there. Thanks also to Cedar and Violet for being badass amazing stepkids. And for enduring a stepmother who curses a lot and writes naughty books.

Thanks especially to Craig, who designs my covers, formats my newsletters, updates my website, makes my toes curl, and sends my heart racing on a regular basis. Love you, hot stuff.

ABOUT THE AUTHOR

When Tawna Fenske finished her English lit degree at 22, she celebrated by filling a giant trash bag full of romance novels and dragging it everywhere until she'd read them all. Now she's a RITA Award finalist, USA Today bestselling author who writes humorous fiction, risqué romance, and heartwarming love stories with a quirky twist. Publishers Weekly has praised Tawna's offbeat romances with multiple starred reviews and noted, "There's something wonderfully relaxing about being immersed in a story filled with over-the-top characters in undeniably relatable situations. Heartache and humor go hand in hand."

Tawna lives in Bend, Oregon, with her husband, step-kids, and a menagerie of ill-behaved pets. She loves hiking, snowshoeing, standup paddleboarding, and inventing excuses to sip wine on her back porch. She can peel a banana with her toes and loses an average of twenty pairs of eyeglasses per year. To find out more about Tawna and her books, visit www.tawnafenske.com.

ALSO BY TAWNA FENSKE

The Ponderosa Resort Romantic Comedy Series

Studmuffin Santa

Chef Sugarlips

Sergeant Sexypants

Hottie Lumberjack

Stiff Suit

Mancandy Crush (novella)

Captain Dreamboat

Snowbound Squeeze (novella)

Dr. Hot Stuff (coming soon!)

The Juniper Ridge Romantic Comedy Series

Show Time

Let It Show (coming March 2021!)

Standalone Romantic Comedies

The Two-Date Rule

At the Heart of It

This Time Around

Now That It's You

Let it Breathe

About That Fling

Frisky Business

Believe It or Not

Making Waves

Made in the USA
Columbia, SC
25 October 2020